# The Betrayal

Mary Parsons

ISBN: 0615545920
ISBN-13: 978-0615545929

# DEDICATION

To the memory of 9/11/01

# ACKNOWLEDGMENTS

9/11/01 was a date of great tragedy for the world. This book is a work of fiction and 9/11 is used as a backdrop in the plot line. My descriptions of events is entirely fictional and not intended to be historically accurate. Please forgive any liberties taken with actual details of that horrible day.

1

Anna almost didn't answer the phone. It was a busy Tuesday morning and she was getting the children organized for a play date with their friend Jennifer. But, Anna thought, Tom is travelling and it might be important. She picked up the phone. At first she heard nothing then suddenly it was Tom's voice. The line was crackling and Anna could barely hear the words.

"Anna...something horrible is going to happen. I love you and the kids so much...please forgive me...."

Before Anna could say anything the line went dead. Tom was on a flight to California. What did he mean? Forgive him for what?

Within a minute or two the phone rang again and she grabbed for the receiver. "Tom?"

"No honey...it's Mother. Is your television on?"

Anna could feel a blanket of doom descending on the room.

"No. Why? "

"Anna....I want you to turn on the news and try to stay calm...I'm coming over."

Anna went into the den and picked up the remote. Her hands shook as she pressed the power button and images of crashing planes leaped onto the screen. It took a moment for her to understand that it was planes crashing into the Twin Towers in New York. The crawler at the bottom of the screen said that they were United Flight 175 and American Flight 11 from Boston.

When Tom travelled, they kept copy of his itinerary on the refrigerator. As Anna walked into the kitchen she could see the paper but her eyes failed to focus on the words.

The paper was affixed with a photo magnet-a photo of Anna and the twins. Tom had told her that he wanted to use that magnet because it reminded him of the reasons he had to come home. This couldn't be happening. She closed her eyes and tried to forestall the moment when her deepest fear would be confirmed.

Finally Anna took a deep breath and looked at the paper. There it was in black and white-American Flight 11 from Boston to Los Angeles. The image of her holding her daughters was inches above the information that meant that their Father was dead.

Unthinkable but there it was. This was the horrible thing. He had called from one of the doomed planes. She returned to the den and collapsed into a chair.

Tom was dead. No one would survive that crash. The images played on the screen but she stopped being able to hear the voices.

Suddenly she realized that her twin daughters, Miriam and Hannah, had walked into the room and were looking d i r e c t l y at the television.

They were just three years old so they could not know that they were watching film of their Daddy dying. Just as Anna started to say something to her daughters, she heard the front door open and her Mother's voice in the hallway.

"Granny..." the girls cried in unison and took off down the hall.

Although she could hear activity in the kitchen, Anna couldn't seem to get up from the chair. When she finally was able to stand, her feet were heavy and she felt like she was walking through a thick blanket-like fog. She held onto the walls as she crept the short distance to the kitchen.

"I thought we were going to Jennifer's? Granny says that we aren't going." Hannah said.

"Not today...we'll go another time...OK?" Anna had no idea how she had the strength to even say that much. She watched gratefully as her Mother shepherded the girls to their bedroom and settled them in front of "Beauty and the Beast".

Anna's mother took her by the arm and led her out into the hallway. When they were out of earshot of the girls, Anna said, "He called me from the plane and said something horrible was going to happen....I didn't know what he meant."

"I know... I know dear...how could you know? Let's sit down for a minute...I'll make tea."

Why did people always think that tea was the solution? Anna had just become a widow and the television was showing the crash over and over. She was watching her husband die over and over. How would tea help her now? But she knew she couldn't rage at her Mother. The poor woman was just trying to help in a situation that was unprecedented.

There was no manual for what to do if a terrorist attack kills your daughter's husband. Emily Post didn't have a protocol for this and you couldn't ask Miss Manners so you made a pot of tea. Not necessarily an unreasonable response.

Anna could see that her Mother's hands were shaking as she poured the tea. Ruth pulled out the chair next to Anna and sat down. They were like two statues looking at each other but not really seeing. Anna's eyes were filled with tears but she couldn't seem to cry. She was in a total state of shock.

"Mom...what am I supposed to do? I have to tell the girls but I don't know what to say. This is a time that will change their lives forever. From now on everything will be either before Daddy died or after Daddy died. The words are so important. "

"I know...you don't have to tell them right now. Let's try to get some more information."

"Mom...I can't watch the television....every time they show the crashes, I see him dying over and over. He was on Flight 11. Oh Mom....he called me and he knew he was going to die...."

"Yes...it was good he was able to do that...at least you were able to hear his voice one more time."

"I almost didn't pick it up…if I hadn't it would be on voicemail and I could hear it again…but now it is just seconds of words I didn't really understand and before I could say anything he was gone."

At that moment the phone rang again and her mother reached to pick it up. Her mother spoke in a whisper and after a few more minutes of quiet conversation, her mother hung up the phone and told Anna that her sister, Rachel, was on her way to Boston.

"I don't want her here." Anna snapped.

"I told her that it was not a good time but she's coming anyway. You know she will. Rachel doesn't listen…she never has."

Anna barely acknowledged her mother's remark. Yes, she thought. Rachel is my twin sister and I know exactly how this will play out. She will sweep in here and make this her own private tragedy. The fact that I lost my husband and my girls lost their Daddy will be secondary to whatever Rachel finds important.

Having her twin in her house was exactly what Anna did not want to happen but Rachel was a force unto herself and if she decided to be here, she would be.

2

Rachel and Anna's were identical twins but that was where the similarity ended. Rachel was a wild child-vastly different from the sedate, thoughtful Anna. Even as children, they had never been close.

They grew up in an English Tudor house on a tree lined street in Brookline. Their Mother, Ruth, worked as a nurse at Newton Wellesley Hospital and their Father, David, had his own practice as a CPA. On the surface, it was gentrified and boringly normal but underneath, there was a layer of discontent and turmoil.

The girls went to an exclusive private school where for every rule Anna obeyed Rachel disobeyed two. The school uniform of a grey pleated skirt, white blouse and a blue blazer was reassuring to Anna and a challenge to Rachel whose skirts would be rolled up so high that her underwear showed.

On several occasions, someone told Anna that they were sure that Rachel did not wear panties. If this was meant to shock Anna it did not have the desired effect. Anna already knew that Rachel went "commando". Anna had no idea where her sister had learned such a thing but she did know that her twin got some sort of thrill out of trying to shock.

But what Rachel didn't understand was that her sister had stopped being shocked years before. Now what Anna felt was pity for her sister who flew in the face of convention and propriety. It was painful to watch and it took a terrible toll on their family life.

Rachel's inappropriate behavior at school was just a microcosm of the chaos in their household. There was endless drama as Rachel flaunted her ill manners and stomped on every sensibility of the family.

Ruth and David wanted their daughters to have a happy childhood but they couldn't seem to reach Rachel. As soon as she had been able to communicate, Rachel had expressed her disapproval of just about everything and everyone. She also ascribed to the rule that if she wasn't happy no one should be happy.

"Too many rules" was the rallying cry as Anna watched her twin do pretty much as she pleased. Ruth cried and spent thousands of dollars on therapists. Rachel would go to the appointments and sit mulishly in a chair until the time was up. At the beginning, the therapist would give Ruth a referral to a colleague but after a while, they even stopped doing that. It was an exercise in futility and a colossal waste of money so Ruth eventually gave up.

During their high school years, Rachel brought an endless parade of unsuitable young men into the house. Little did these young men know that they were pawns Rachel's game of Shock the Parents. Each one was just a little worse than the one before. If tattoos failed to shock, the next one would have facial piercings but to her parent's credit they developed a very high tolerance for these misfits and did admirably in concealing their revulsion.

The truth was that it wasn't the physical appearance of the boys that bothered Ruth and David; it was the fact that Rachel was sexually active and appeared to be quite promiscuous. Ruth had found her birth control pills and an envelope of condoms so at least Rachel seemed to be practicing safe sex but it still grieved her parents that she would have such loose morals.

During this time, Anna had the usual teenage dates to the movies and parties. The young men she dated were the exact opposite of the peculiar assortment chosen by her sister.

These were young men with expensively styled hair, preppy clothing and cultivated voices who went to expensive private schools and aspired to be accepted at whatever Ivy League school his family favored.

Of course, the boys had the usual teenage hormones and had heard rumors about Rachel but they soon learned that Anna had very different standards. Although she would allow kissing and some casual necking, Anna refused further physical intimacy.

Whenever she was tempted to go further than kissing and fondling, she thought of the vacant expression on her sister's face. Rachel had navigated her way through dozens of eager young men but if you looked past her tough exterior, there was an emotional void.

Rachel pushed the envelope with her antisocial behavior but she never neglected her schoolwork. She was always at the top of the class which was probably the reason she was allowed to stay at their exclusive school. The head master would excuse her brazen behavior in order to be able to showcase her academic excellence.

When it was time for college, Rachel made almost perfect scores on her SATs. She was approached by every Ivy League school in New England but Rachel had no interest in staying close to home. She applied for early admittance at Stanford and was immediately accepted.

Anna also had impressive SAT scores but she did not want to be far away from home. She was accepted at Simmons College, a few miles from home and breathed a sigh of relief when they took her twin to the airport for her flight to California. Finally she would be able to have a life. It would no longer be a weird half-life with her evil twin lurking in the background just waiting to embarrass her in front of her friends.

Once Anna was in California, she returned only for brief visits. It always appeared that she was doing well in school but her physical appearance had become increasingly disturbing. Her once lush brown hair was cut extremely short and her large brown eyes had become sunken and dull. She obviously was not eating properly, if at all. Ruth and David were at a loss. Rachel had never listened to their advice and it seemed unlikely that she was going to start now.

The visits were always tense. Rachel went out every night and rarely got out of bed before dinner time. There was little time for any actual talk.

Anna was grateful to be ignored. She had her own friends and she had met Tom Weiss. He asked her to dance at a mixer at Harvard and she was head over heels in love with him. Tom was handsome, kind and very intelligent but most of all she liked him. She loved the fact that he had nice manners and was interested in listening to her opinions. It reminded her of the type of relationship her parents enjoyed.

Because Tom was an only child, he was fascinated that Anna had an identical twin. Anna tried to modulate her description of her sister but it was difficult to find positive things to say.

The most truthful way to describe her twin was to talk about her intelligence. Anna felt that it sounded shallow to continually tell Tom that her twin sister was smart but what else was there to say? She couldn't tell him that her sister was a tramp who used drugs and drank heavily. It was never openly discussed in her family but everyone knew the truth. There had been enough drunken calls and several occasions when the police brought Rachel home after finding her staggering around the neighborhood. Even now, there were calls from California and hushed conversations about some sort of trouble with Rachel. Anna never asked her parents about Rachel's escapades. Why would she want to know?

Tom knew there had to be a reason that Rachel was rarely mentioned but he was too polite to ask. When he spoke to David about proposing to Anna, there was a short, vague discussion of "problems" with Rachel but that was the extent of the information made available to him.

Rachel received a degree from Stanford and was hired by a startup company in Palo Alto. According to what they were told, Rachel was some sort of computer genius and she was situated smack in the middle of Silicon Valley.

Anna and Tom married the summer after graduation. Rachel was so engrossed in her work that she "forgot" to come to the wedding. When Ruth told Anna that Rachel had "missed" the flight they had arranged for her, Anna wanted to dance a jig. Her sister's absence was the nicest thing that Rachel had ever done for her twin. Naturally, Anna feigned disappointment that her sister was not able to attend her wedding but anyone close to the family breathed a heavy sigh of relief that Anna's wedding would not be spoiled by Rachel.

Anna and Tom moved into an apartment near Coolidge Corner in Brookline. They both were in graduate programs and it was an easy commute for each of them. Ruth told them about Rachel's triumphs in California but Anna had no direct contact with her twin. For Tom, there was a mystique about Rachel and he found it curious that Anna showed no interest in her twin's life.

Hannah and Miriam were born on Anna and Tom's second wedding anniversary. Rachel sent them a generous check and an impersonal note of congratulations. It wasn't until David died, that Tom met Rachel. It was a somber time and against all odds, Rachel's behavior was entirely appropriate and subdued. She stayed a week to sit Shiva with Ruth and then flew back to California without a backward glance.

Tom couldn't understand why the family whispered about Rachel and her antisocial behavior. He had found her to be charming although he did find it surreal to see another version of his wife. Anna and Rachel had a strong resemblance but the years had hardened Rachel's look. That was the only hint that some of the stories about her lifestyle might be true.

The day after Rachel left, Tom finally found the courage to bring up the subject. He and Anna were finishing coffee after dinner and he said, "It was nice that Rachel was able to be here."

The moment he said the name, he could see Anna's jaw clamp shut. "Well...her father died, I should hope that she would make the trip and try to behave like a human being for a change."

Tom put up his hand in a gesture of peace and said, "Anna....I just mentioned it...no need to be defensive. I've heard so much about her and this is the first time I met her. I was wondering what all the fuss was about."

"I know...she's a master manipulator and she played you like a two dollar banjo. Tom, please believe me when I say that it will be better for our family if she has no contact. It will only end in tears."

"OK..." was the only thing Tom could think of to say.

That had been almost two years ago. The company Rachel worked for went public and she made a ridiculous amount of money before deciding that she was moving east to go to medical school.

For the past year she had been living in Baltimore and there did not seem to be as much drama in her life or at least nothing Anna heard about.

Then about six months ago, Ruth received an e-mail. Rachel said that she was pregnant. The only mention of paternity was to say that the father would not be involved in parenting.

So now Rachel was on her way to Boston to unload her pack of troubles into Anna's already fractured house. How did she even know Tom was on a flight to California? Anna had an uneasy feeling that there was something larger going on. And if Rachel was involved it would end badly. It always did.

3

When Rabbi Ben Cantor arrived about an hour later, Anna met him at the door.

"Good morning Rabbi. Please come in."

Rabbi Cantor stepped into the foyer, closed the door and then reached out to hug Anna. She tried to back away but before she knew it, she was enveloped by his arms. The wool of his suit scratched her cheek and she could smell the cloying scent of his after shave. It was suffocating and just as she thought he would crush her to death, he pulled away and she was left shaking from the experience.

Her mother came into the hallway and he said, "Ruth...thank you for calling me. It's a terrible tragedy."

Anna watched as the Rabbi and her mother shared an awkward hug. Why she had never noticed that the Rabbi was not very good at hugging. She trailed along behind them as they went into the living room where Ruth had set up a tea tray.

"Ben, thank you for coming so soon...we know you're busy. I didn't know what to do...we have so much to think about. We have to tell the girls and it's all over the television."

Ben considered this for a moment and said, "I'll help you tell the children. I don't know how much of the details you need to tell them right now. Just that Daddy's plane crashed and he won't be coming back."

Her mother and Ben looked over at Anna for agreement. She was huddled in an upholstered chair with absolutely no discernible expression on her face.

"Anna....honey...did you hear Ben?"

No response. Ruth went over and knelt in front of the chair. When she touched her daughter's hand it was ice cold. Now Ruth started to become really concerned. "Anna...can you hear us?"

There was the hint of a nod but nothing else changed in her demeanor. Anna seemed to be suspended in time. Ruth looked over her shoulder at Ben and said, "It's the shock...we need to wrap something around her and get her to drink some tea. She'll come around in a minute."

Anna could hear Ruth's words and thought....no I won't. I'm never going to be back in the same world again. It's gone. I have two fatherless children and I have to make them cry. I have to be strong and I'm not. They have to hear this from me.

The silence in the room was overwhelming. Ruth found a pink alpaca wool shawl to wrap around Anna's shoulders. When she tried to get Anna to drink tea, the response was a violent shake of her head. "No tea."

Neither the Rabbi nor Ruth dared to say anything more. There was something about the look in her eyes that made them fearful that she was having a break with reality.

Anna wondered the same thing but then she thought about the girls. They had lost one parent today and she needed to be strong. She could almost hear Tom whispering in her ear...I'm sorry...I love you.

Suddenly Anna rose from her chair, looked at her Mother and Ben and said, "Excuse me...I have to go break my children's hearts." With that, she walked slowly out of the room and down the hall to her daughters' bedroom. They heard the door close and the television noise stopped.

"Do you think I should go down there?" Ruth asked.

"No...this is private...she'll ask if she needs our help."

Ruth said, "I haven't been able to watch television. Do you know more about what happened?"

"Terrorism. Two planes into the Trade Center towers, one into the Pentagon and one into a field in Pennsylvania.

"A field in Pennsylvania?"

"Yes, the passengers knew that the hijackers were going to crash it in Washington so they stopped it. Some very brave people there."

"Tom called Anna from the plane and told her something horrible was going to happen. Ben, he knew he was going to die and he called to say goodbye."

"Well...that should be some comfort..."

Ruth interrupted and said, "She wishes it had gone to voice mail so she could listen to it again..."

Ben pondered that for a moment and said, "I can understand that."

Before Ruth could say more, they heard the door open and the sound of six feet walking down the hallway. They entered the room hand in hand.

The girls were dressed in flowered jumpers and leggings. Their tiny feet were encased in sandals and multi-colored barrettes held their abundant, curly hair. The twins clung to Anna as if she were a helium balloon they were afraid would float way.

"Ben. The girls would like to talk with you. Mother, maybe you could make some more tea. I need to lie down for a few minutes."

Ruth said, "Come on girls, come sit here and you can have a cookie."

The girls looked up at their mother who nodded for them to go to their Granny. Slowly dropping their mother's hands, the twins walked reluctantly away from Anna.

As soon as they seemed focused on Ben and her mother, Anna turned and walked to her bedroom. When she entered the room she was immediately aware of the lingering scent of Tom's after shave. Only a few hours before he had been standing in this bedroom, buttoning his shirt and telling her about the new project in California.

They had just made love and Anna was lolling about in sheets that were still warm from his body. She had been half listening as he explained that he was moving on from the project he had been working in Washington, DC. In a haze of sexual bliss, Anna heard the words but her concentration was on admiring her husband's slim body. Now she wished she had listened more about the trip.

As she walked further into the room, the scent became stronger and suddenly she was overcome with nausea. Running to the bathroom, she barely made it to the toilet before the contents of her stomach emptied and she was left heaving on the floor. Why bother to get up, she thought and rested her face on the cool, ceramic floor tile.

Ben was waiting for the twins to speak. So far, they had each eaten a cookie and now they were sitting quietly staring at the floor. It was obvious that there had been tears but now they had no expression on their faces. Eerie to look at three year olds who look so solemn, thought Ben.

He finally broke the silence but asking, "Did your Mommy tell you what happened to your Daddy."

Almost as one the little girls nodded but did not say a word.

Ben pushed on, "Do you want to talk about it?

Hannah was the talkative one and she finally said, "No...we want our Daddy to come back."

"Did Mommy tell you that he can't come back?"

"Yes." said Hannah, "But I think he could if he wanted to."

Miriam whispered, "Where do Daddies go when they can't come back? He was here this morning. He said he would be back on Friday and bring us presents."

Ben said, "He is in a place where he will always be able to see you. He didn't want to go...it is a terrible thing that happened."

The girls starting crying again and Hannah asked, "Will he be lonely there?"

"No, sweetheart but he will miss you. He will always miss you. He is OK and there are other Daddies there. I think they keep each other company."

Ruth was in the kitchen and she could feel her heart breaking a little more with each word. There was a silence for a moment and she peeked into the room. The girls looked at her and Hannah said, "Granny, we need to see Mommy."

Before Ruth could say a word, they jumped down from their chairs and ran down the hallway in the direction of their mother's room. It was few minutes later that they heard the girls calling for their mother.

A sense of panic rose in Ruth as she tore down the hallway and burst into the bedroom. She could see that they girls were standing next to each other peering into the bathroom. The bile rose in her throat as she said, "Anna?"

Hannah looked at Ruth and said, "She won't get up."

Ruth looked into the bathroom and saw Anna sprawled on the floor next to the toilet. She was white as a ghost and Ruth immediately feared the worst. Just as she was going to scream for Ben, Anna moved. She picked up her head, saw her mother and the girls and said, "It's OK...Mommy just felt sick." She rose from the floor, went to the sink, washed her face and rinsed her mouth. "I'm sorry girls, let's go in and lie down on Mommy's bed."

Anna took the twins' hands and they moved across the room to the bed. After a little maneuvering, she lay down between the girls and they curled up together. Ruth floated a comforter over them and left the room.

Back in the living room, Ben was fingering his pager. He looked up absently and said, "Is she OK? I just heard that there is another member who was killed on one of the planes so I will have to go there. This tragedy will go on and on...I've never know such a thing."

Ruth said, "They're sleeping which is probably for the best. Rachel will be here later."

That was eyebrow raising news for Ben. Rachel rarely visited and for her to make the effort right now seemed odd. She wasn't a family oriented person and had never shown the slightest interest in her nieces. Maybe it was just the bizarre, tragic events of the day-it wasn't charitable to be suspicious of Rachel but....even so, he just had a bad feeling about what would happen during the visit.

After Ben left, Ruth made another cup of tea and sat down to watch the news. Anna had been right- it was like watching Tom die over and over but it was mesmerizing and she couldn't look away.

It was several hours later when Anna appeared in front of her. "Mother, please turn that off."

Ruth felt guilty and ashamed as she reached for the remote control. "I'm sorry dear....I wanted to find out if they had anything new to report."

"Will that make a difference?" snapped Anna. Her face was still pale and her jaw was clamped so tight Ruth could see the muscles poking out.

"No dear but...I wanted to know. I'm not going to apologize for wanting to know how something this terrible could happen."

Anna's face calmed slightly and she said, "I'm sorry....I just can't watch...not now. You have every right to the information if it will help you. Go ahead...I am going back in to check on the girls."

As Anna left the room, Ruth realized that she had no idea what was going through her daughter's head. She was used to that with Rachel and after all the escapades in California, she was actually grateful to not know what Rachel was thinking but, Anna had always been open and able to share her feelings. Now she had retreated to a dark, unknown place and Ruth feared that she might never return.

4

It was late afternoon when the doorbell rang and Ruth found
Rachel standing on the front steps. She was dressed in a loose tunic
and leggings. Her swollen belly strained at the seams of the tunic-
she was very pregnant indeed.

Ruth opened the door. "Come in....how was your trip?"

Rachel seemed to be distracted and was looking furtively
around the hallway. "Where's Anna?" she whispered.

"Resting with the girls."

"Oh." Rachel said as she walked down the hallway towards
the master bedroom.

Ruth fought back the impulse to question Rachel's motives. A
few minutes later, Anna appeared in the doorway with a look of
panic in her eyes.

"Did you see Rachel?" Ruth asked.

"Yes. She barged into my room and started rooting around in Tom's closet. She's pulling all the clothes off the hangers. Mother...please stop her."

Ruth was instantly sorry that she had not stopped Rachel from going into Anna's room. "Where are the girls?"

"In their room...I bribed them with a video again."

"Good..." said Ruth as she stalked from the room. How could Rachel be so insensitive?

When Ruth entered the bedroom, it took her a minute to find Rachel. When she did, she was horrified to find her sitting on the floor of the walk-in closet surrounded by a pile of Tom's clothes. She was holding a shirt up to her face and crying.

Walking towards her, Ruth could see row after row of empty hangers and a huge pile of clothing on the floor.

"Rachel...what are you doing?"

Rachel slowly pulled her face away from the shirt and looked pathetically at Ruth.

Ruth knelt down next to Rachel, "What is this about?"

"He's gone." Rachel sniffed. "I won't see him again."

Ruth held her daughter's hand and said, "I know. We will miss him but...Rachel, this is your sister's home and her husband's clothes. You can't just go through his things. You need to be here for Anna and the girls. This is not about you."

Rachel gave Ruth a crazed look and said, "Yes it is....it's always about me. It has to be about me. He abandoned me."

Ruth had no idea what Rachel was saying but she knew that this was not good..."He left all of us. Please, you need to pull yourself together. Let me clean this up. Wash your face and go see your sister."

Ruth watched as Rachel's head started to loll forward and her eyes closed as she whispered, "I don't mean today."

Ruth looked down at Rachel's hands and that was when she saw the brown pill bottle.

Ruth was a retired nurse and she knew that this was very serious. Just as she was about to run for the telephone, Anna appeared in the doorway and Ruth said, "Anna....call 911...she's taken pills."

Anna hesitated for a split second and Ruth raised her voice..."Now...Anna...now."

Ruth tried to move Rachel but with the pregnancy weight, she was too heavy. Instead, she went and drenched towels with cold water and placed them on Rachel's neck. She knew that she needed to try to keep her from going further into unconsciousness.

When she looked down at the area where Rachel had been lying, she saw the wet stain on the floor. Looking more closely at Rachel, she saw that her legs were wet-her water had broken.

The paramedics worked fast and within minutes, Rachel was on her way to the hospital. Ruth looked at Anna and said, "I hate to leave you."

"Mother, she's your daughter too.  We'll be OK."

When Ruth walked into the emergency room she could see people working on Rachel. She identified herself and a woman with a clipboard took her aside.

There were questions and Ruth had very few answers. No… she didn't know the name of Rachel's doctor. No… she didn't know the due date. No…she didn't know about insurance. Yes…she was Rachel's mother but…Rachel lived out of state and had only come to Boston tonight. After a few more attempts to get information, the woman started tapping away on the computer keyboard. "OK…we'll let you know if we have any other questions and maybe you could arrange to have some answers."

Ruth swallowed her anger and went over to a bank of plastic chairs where she slumped into a seat. She buried her head in her hands and wept. This was a nightmare.

Through her tears she saw a pair of black shoes approaching. More questions, she thought and tried to regain control enough to talk to another stranger.

When she looked up, she saw that it was Jerry Miller, her friend and lover. She had thought he was out of town.

"Jerry...what are you doing here?"

"Anna called me."

Jerry pulled Ruth up from the chair and held her tightly in his arms. "I'm so sorry about all this. I'll be right here for you."

Ruth melted into his body and whispered, "I thought you were away."

"I was but with everything that happened I drove back this afternoon. I had only been home a few minutes when Anna called."

"Did she tell you about Tom?"

"I heard from Ben. I called him this afternoon and he told me about Tom. I didn't know about this thing with Rachel until Anna called."

Jerry and Ben had been friends for years, and their wives had been very close until Jerry's wife, Rebecca, had died three years ago. When David died about a year later, Ben had encouraged Jerry to spend time with Ruth. They were drawn together by grief but their close friendship gradually melted into love and now they were devoted to each other.

"What's happening here?"

Ruth shook her head and said, "I don't know. She's pregnant and she's taken pills. She showed up on Anna's doorstep talking incoherently about Tom abandoning her. I don't know what it all means but...Jerry...it's very bad..."

Jerry drew her closer and they held each other until they heard the sound of footsteps approaching. Drawing apart, they saw a young man dressed in a white coat headed in their direction. He had a stethoscope around his neck and a worried expression on his face.

"Are you Rachel's parents?"

Ruth almost laughed over the assumption that had been made and said, "I'm her mother."

"I'm Dr. Levine. We're taking Rachel upstairs now to deliver the baby. We've pumped her stomach and she is semi-conscious but the baby has to be delivered soon. I have to go and scrub up. We will let you know when we have more news."

Before they could ask any more questions, he turned and headed in the direction of a bank of elevators. A group of scrub clad people were pushing a gurney where Rachel lay motionless. There was a fetal monitor strapped across her belly and from the number of tubes and beeping machines surrounding her, Ruth could tell that this was a very grave situation. She had to look away. Jerry put his arm around her and steered her back to the chairs.

"Why is this happening?" Ruth cried.

"I don't know. It's a terrible day and it's not over yet. We have to be strong for the girls and each other. I'm going to call Ben and let him know."

Jerry stepped away and Ruth could hear him talking softly on the phone. When he returned to Ruth's side he said, "Ben will be here in a little while."

## 6

Anna paced the floor. She had fed the girls macaroni and cheese before giving them a bath with an extravagant amount of bubbles. They had been silent as they picked at their food and even more silent in their bath. Even the added treat of extra bubble bath did not cheer them tonight. Now they were now tucked into her bed. No one would be sleeping alone tonight.

She wondered what was happening at the hospital and what it all meant. She remembered the call from Tom. He had said that he was sorry but what was he sorry about? Why did she have this nagging feeling that everything was somehow related?

Why had Rachel come into her room with a crazed look on her face and start rummaging through Tom's clothes? Rachel had been moaning but Anna hadn't been able to make out any words. What had she been saying?

The telephone rang and she jumped to pick it up.

"Hello." "Anna...it's Mother. They've taken Rachel up to deliver the baby....it very bad. I don't know when I will be back. Are you going to be OK there alone?"

"Yes. I'll put on a movie...the girls are sleeping."

"OK." Ruth hung up the pay phone and absently wondered where she had left her cell phone. She couldn't even remember the last time she saw it.

Jerry found a coffeemaker and they sat silently sipping the stale, acrid brown liquid. About an hour later, Dr. Levine returned wearing scrubs and looking very strained.

"Well...I just delivered a baby boy. He's a little over six pounds but he has had a hard time. We have him in Neonatal Intensive Care...we will know more in a couple of hours."

"How is my daughter?"

"She lost a lot of blood and there were complications. We had to do a hysterectomy. Someone is finishing that up right now and then she will be in ICU. It may be a long recovery for her and we have to address her mental state as well. Do you know anything about that?"

"No...she lives out of state and I haven't seen her in a few months. She's in medical school in Baltimore."

"The nurses said that she kept crying for someone named Tom...do you know who that is?"

Ruth's heart fell. "Tom is her twin sister's husband-he was on one of the planes that hit the Trade Center this morning."

Dr. Levine's face clouded and he said, "My God, what a lot of tragedy. We'll keep you posted."

Jerry and Ruth watched the doctor retreat into the depths of the hospital. Before Ruth could say anything, Jerry put his hand on her shoulder and said, "Let's not jump to any conclusions."

"Jerry...it's something she said. She told me that Tom had abandoned her and I tried to say that he abandoned everyone but then she said, that she didn't mean today. Those were her exact words....not today. Oh Jerry, she had gone into Tom's closet and ripped all the clothes off the hangers and lay there to kill herself and the baby. What am I supposed to think?"

"I don't know but...let's try to focus on what's happening now. It's going to be a long night and you still have to be There for Anna and the girls so....let's try to stay in the present for now.

Deep down inside, Ruth knew he was right but the dread and panic was lurking in her consciousness; ready to spring into action at any moment. It was easy to say that she should focus on the present but....there was something going on here that would add another dimension to the grief and pain of this terrible day. Their lives would be destroyed and as the Mother she would have to try to pick up the pieces. That's what Mothers do.

## 7

Anna had decided to watch "Keeping the Faith", a romantic comedy with Ben Stiller and Edward Norton. It was one of her favorite movies but Tom classified it as a "chick flick" so she only watched it when he was not there. Well...she thought bitterly...I don't have to worry about that any more.

The telephone had been ringing on and off all day. The doorbell had rung a couple of times but she was ignoring everything. What she wanted was for the world to fall away from her so she and the girls could grieve without the world watching.

That's what she wanted but she knew it wouldn't happen. Her husband had been killed in a spectacular terrorist attack and her heartbreak would be public. But for now, she just wanted to cherish the quiet of the moment. As usual, Rachel had burst onto the scene with her craziness and grabbed her Mother away.

Her grandmother would have said... Twas ever thus, thought Anna.

Rachel had been born first and had always demanded the limelight and attention. She was never satisfied to be in the background-she sucked all the air out a room. The only way Anna seemed to be able to get any attention was to be the polar opposite so that's what she did. Anna was studious, thoughtful and dependable while her sister cut a swath of chaos through the world. So it was no surprise that Rachel would show up today with a pack of troubles and empty it in Anna's house.

The video was playing but, Ana was only half listening and not really watching at all. She could see lights outside the house and the doorbell rang. She peeked out from behind a curtain and saw that her driveway was full of reporters.

When they saw her face the cameras starting flashing and she realized that image would probably appear in the paper. These people were ghouls who were trying to see her pain- they would rejoice in her grief because, to them, it was news. How would she survive this?

Ruth and Jerry sat in the waiting room hoping that someone would come to them with news. After what seemed to be an eternity (but was really about two hours) a nurse came to them and said that Rachel was in ICU. She was stable and the baby was improving. She told them there was a waiting room in ICU and asked if they wanted to see the baby.

For the first time in hours, Ruth felt her heart open to a spark of joy. New life amid the tragedy. It had to be a sign of hope.

They followed the nurse through the hallways and into an area where a large glassed window separated them from a nursery full of machine, lights and nurses. In little incubators, lay babies attached to tubes and monitors. Some of them were hardly bigger than a small bird but they were struggling to live. In the back, near a door was the incubator with Rachel's name....baby boy Markowitz.

The nurse helped Ruth gown up and ushered her into the room. Just about the only noise the sound of monitors and machines. The nurses moved about quietly caring for the babies.

Ruth put her hands through the ports on the side of the incubator and she was able to touch the delicate skin of her new grandson. Although she was wearing gloves, she could feel the warmth of his skin and in response to her touch he turned his head and looked at her.

"I'm your Granny, little man. We need to get you a name. Be strong because right now your mommy is sick. I love you." She withdrew her hands and the nurse led her out of the room.

"We'll be trying to feed him soon. Would you like to hold him for his first bottle? He's doing well and can be out of the incubator for a few minutes. Usually we would try to get his mother down here but I'm told she is recovering from surgery."

Ruth was crying now and said, "I will be here for every feeding. Just say the word. You've been very kind."

"Well... he needs to bond. He'll be out in the normal nursery tomorrow. Considering the stress of his birth, he's doing very well. "

"Will I be able to see my daughter?"

"I'll make a call and find out."

Ruth stood with Jerry and neither said a word.  That was one of the things she loved about this man-he knew when to be quiet.  The nurse returned and told them that they should go to ICU and someone would talk to them there.

8

Ruth leaned onto Jerry as they walked through the maze of hallways towards ICU. The feeling of joy had evaporated and had been replaced by the familiar sense of dread always associated with Rachel. How often had she been in the position to unravel the aftermath of Rachel's insensitivity and selfishness?

Her husband had been an enabler for Rachel. David always had an explanation for Rachel's bizarre, antisocial behavior and when she tearfully apologized, he believed her when she promised that it would never happen again.

David was Rachel's champion and savior. Now, with him gone, Rachel's erratic behavior was Ruth's burden. At this moment she felt overwhelmed by the responsibility.

Ruth knew that this was not the average Rachel misadventure. There was something horribly hurtful about this whole episode. Whatever was happening with Rachel would overshadow the unimaginable tragedy of Tom's death. It seemed impossible that anything could be more earthshattering but....Ruth just had a feeling.

At the door of ICU they were met by a solemn looking young man who identified himself as Dr. Willis.

"I'm a psychiatrist. Your daughter is coming out of the anesthesia and I need to ask you some questions-are you her next of kin?"

"I'm her mother."

"Good, let's sit down over here and we can talk." He looked at Jerry and said, "Are you her father?"

Jerry shook his head and said, "No, I am a friend of the family."

Dr. Willis looked at Ruth and said, "Do you want to talk privately?"

"No...Jerry is a dear friend and I would like to have him with me."

They moved into a lounge area and sat down on uncomfortable, worn sofas. There was a coffee maker in the corner and Dr. Willis gestured towards the machine and asked, "Would you like a cup of coffee?"

Ruth looked at the dark brown liquid pooled in the pot and said, "No...I don't think so."

"Probably a wise choice. Now...Mrs. Markowitz, your daughter took an overdose of a powerful tranquilizer. If you hadn't been there, she and the baby would have died. Have you ever known her to be suicidal?"

Ruth didn't know where to start. "Dr. Willis, my daughter has lived in another part of the country since she was 18 years old. I can't say that I know much about her medical history except for the fact that she has taken antidepressant medication on and off for years. She has had periods of stopping the medications and there have always been problems. I have no knowledge of suicidal thoughts but....I wouldn't rule it out. Rachel has always had problems. She's brilliant and has been successful but it has come at the cost of estranging her from her family. Today was the first time I have seen her in almost a year."

"OK....I was told that she is in medical school. The prescription bottle was from a pharmacy in Baltimore, Do you know about that?"

"She just started her third year at Johns Hopkins. We stay in touch by e-mail and she hasn't mentioned anything."

"I have a call into the doctor who prescribed the drug. Rachel was irrational when she was admitted and we need to address that. Something precipitated this suicide attempt. If she is in medical school she certainly knew what it meant to the baby. If anything had happened to the baby we could be dealing with criminal charges."

Ruth gasped and her hand flew up to her mouth. That had never occurred to her but...he was right.

Jerry put his arm around her shoulders and said, "Dr. Willis, we have been told that the baby is doing quite well and right now Ruth is caught between seeing to Rachel and seeing to her other daughter who lost her husband today. There are three year old twins who have no father and a new baby who has a mother who tried to kill him before he was born. I think that we need to try to minimize the stress here and focus on how we can help Rachel so that Ruth can get back to Anna."

Dr. Willis' expression changed immediately and said, "No one told me, I am so sorry for your loss. Mrs. Markowitz, this can wait. Rachel is sleeping and we will monitor her closely. Please go ahead with whatever you need to do. We'll call you if we need you."

## 9

Ruth sat down in a rocking chair and the nurse handed her
the baby who was swaddled in a blue blanket. Looking at the red,
slightly swollen face of her grandson, she had the oddest feeling. Not
quite déjà vu but something similar.

The nurse gave her a bottle and when she held it near the baby's
mouth, he reached out immediately to drink hungrily. Ruth
rocked as the baby drank and for the first time in hours, she felt a bit
of serenity. There was more to this whole story but for right now,
she was feeding her first grandson and that was enough.

After the baby was changed and put back in his incubator, Ruth
met Jerry and they had something to eat. She had little appetite but
knew that she needed to eat. Her next stop would be Rachel and
she dreaded what that would entail.

Anna could not sleep. Every few minutes she checked on the girls
and found them sleeping peacefully in her bed. Once or twice she
tried lying down with them but she couldn't settle her mind.
Images of Rachel sprawled unconscious on Tom's clothes
constantly flashed into her mind. It reminded her of a slide show on
a perpetual loop. Nothing seemed to clear her mind. Her world had
shattered and her sister had come to stomp on the pieces.

A list, she thought. That was what she needed. A list would help organize her thoughts. She curled up on the sofa and started writing down what she thought needed to be done.

1. Call Rabbi Cantor to arrange Bris.
2. Call Tom's employer.
3. Make appt with pediatrician.
4. Call our lawyer

Making the list was therapeutic and eventually she was able to fall asleep. She was dozing on the sofa when the door opened and her mother walked in with Jerry. Ruth saw that Anna was asleep and she sighed. There would be long days ahead and sleep was the best thing for her right now.

The noise of the door woke Anna and she looked up sleepily.

"Oh dear....what time is it? Are the girls OK?" Ruth stopped her before she leaped from the sofa and said, "Jerry went to check on them. Stay here for the moment."

Jerry came back and said, "Sleeping soundly. I'm going to make some fresh coffee and see if I can rustle up some food....is it OK if I take over your kitchen for a bit?"

Anna looked at him blankly and said, "Of course."

Soon there were sounds of cooking in the kitchen and they could smell the aroma of fresh coffee. Ruth said, "I have had too many cups of stale coffee today. I'm dreaming of a nice mug of coffee." She glanced down at the pad resting on her daughter's lap.

"Making a list? You have always been a list maker. When you were little, if you were upset about something, I would give you a paper and pencil and tell you to make a list. It always seemed to calm you."

Anna smiled weakly and said, "I remember."

"What's first on the list?"

"A Bris for the baby....we will need to do it on the 19th. I'll call the Rabbi."

"You're right but put Jerry in charge of that one. "

" He had life insurance but...there won't be a body...."

Ruth's heart broke as she heard Anna talk so logically and frankly about the details of their life.

"We'll find out for you. I'll help. Now...I want to tell you a little about what happened with Rachel."

At that moment, Jerry walked back in the room with a tray that held two large mugs of coffee and two plates of eggs and toast.

"The best I could do...I have rather limited culinary skills. I'll leave you with this and go check on the girls again.

Ruth picked up the mug of coffee with one hand and the plate of eggs with the other. She rested the plate on her lap as she drank the coffee. "Ah...perfect. Now, honey, you need to eat something...try Jerry's eggs....he's good at making eggs."

Anna wondered why Ruth thought she would be interested in Jerry's culinary skills and then realized that her Mother was just stalling for time.

The food did smell good. She couldn't remember the last time she ate. Anna picked up the plate and scooped some scrambled eggs onto the fork. As soon as the food crossed her lips, she realized that her Mother was right. These eggs were delicious. She took another bite and then another until the plate was empty. Picking up the coffee mug, she sighed and said, "Now tell me what I need to know."

"Well...the baby is going to be OK. He's in neonatal ICU until the morning but he seems to have no ill effects. I had a chance to feed him and he drank the whole bottle. I had forgotten how peaceful it is to feed an infant."

Anna's face became dreamy as she whispered, "I haven't...its lovely."

Ruth went on, "Then we went to see Rachel. They asked me all kinds of questions and I didn't have the answers. They want to know about her mental health. When they were prepping her for surgery, she was very disoriented and combative and they are concerned that she has had some sort of breakdown."

Anna looked at her Mother in a quizzical way and said, "Obviously....look what she did! She came in here looking like a homeless person, tore all of Tom's clothes off the hangers and then tried to kill herself and the baby she was carrying. I hope it was a breakdown because I can't think that it was a conscious act... She's always been crazy...I can't believe that we share the same DNA."

"Anna, Rachel has not always been crazy...this is the first time she has done anything so irrational."

"The first time we know about you mean." snapped Anna.

"OK...let's not go there....she's going to need some help and we have to decide what to do with the baby."

"The baby will come here. I'll have Jerry get one of the cribs down from the attic. The baby can stay here but I'm not having Rachel's brand of crazy coming into this home. I am a widow and my children are fatherless. We have enough crazy coming down the pike for us without my selfish sister."

Ruth looked at Anna and could see from the set of her mouth that there was no use arguing this point. "I understand. She may need to go to a facility anyway. We have to take the suicide attempt seriously."

Anna changed the subject by saying, "Tomorrow I'm going to see the baby."

"Are you sure you want to do that?"

"Yes. Now it is time for me to go in with the girls. I don't want them to wake up alone." Anna rose from the sofa and straightened her shoulders as she calmly walked from the room.

After Ruth heard the bedroom door close, she cleared up the dishes and took the tray back to the kitchen. Jerry was sitting at the table reading the newspaper. Ruth sat down with a sigh and said, "At first I thought she was going to fall to pieces but now I think it may be me."

Jerry took her hand and said, "I won't permit that.

Now...let's find the guest room and get some rest."

Hours later, Ruth woke up in Jerry's arms and snuggled down onto his chest. Jerry stirred and said, "Let's just stay here forever."

Ruth laughed and said, "I know but we have to face it." She got up and dressed in a fluffy peach colored robe that she had found in the closet.

Anna was in the kitchen with the girls who were busily devouring pancakes. They looked up from their plates and smiled at Ruth. She leaned in to each of them and received two lovely sticky kisses. What a nice way to start the morning she thought.

Anna set a cup of coffee in front of Ruth and said,

"Pancakes?"

Ruth shook her head and said, "No thank you. Why don't you go take a shower and get dressed? I'll watch the girls and get them cleaned up. Jerry is going to call the hospital."

"OK...a shower would be nice."

## 10

Later that day, after securing the services of a babysitter, Anna and Ruth drove to the hospital. Baby Boy Markowitz was sound asleep in the regular nursery. A nurse came out and after they explained who they were, she brought the baby to an empty room so they could spend some time with him.

He looked so tiny and vulnerable in his little blue cap. Anna instinctively reached to pick him up. When the baby felt her touch, he opened his eyes and looked directly at Anna.

Ruth could see the look of shock come across her daughter's face. Ruth moved closer and said, "Honey, what it is?"

Anna's voice was hushed and tremulous when she said, "Those are Tom's eyes."

At that moment everything seemed to fall into place for Ruth. That was why she had the strange feeling when the baby looked at her. Rachel's baby had Tom's eyes. Ever since Rachel had said "I don't mean today" she had known...somewhere deep down she had known but now that it was out in the open she was too horrified to speak.

Ruth could feel herself start to shake and Anna reached over to pat her arm. "It's OK."

Anna scooped the baby up and cradled him in her arms. "It's OK little man. I knew your Daddy and he would have loved you. Mother, are you OK?"

Ruth was too overwhelmed to speak. What was there to say?

Anna's voice was clear and even when she said, "It's going to be alright. We'll work this out somehow. Tom would want me to...he would never had meant for the baby to suffer because of Rachel. He never understood about Rachel....he trusted her."

Anna was rocking the baby in her arms and softly crooning a song. At first, Ruth couldn't identify it but then in a flash, she realized that it was a lullaby-the same one she had sung to Anna and Rachel so many years ago.

Ruth stood up to leave and Anna looked up calmly, "I'm staying with the baby. You go see Rachel."

As Ruth approached the door of room, she could see Rachel lying in the bed with her face to the wall. A nurse was adjusting one of the IV lines and she greeted Ruth with a smile. "Come on in. I'm almost done."

"Thank you.  How is she?"

As soon as the words were out of Ruth's mouth she saw Rachel's head snap around. Her eyes were clouded but very Intense as she hissed, "Ask me...I'm right here."

The nurse shrugged her shoulders and left the room.  Ruth walked over and stood next to the bed.  Rachel's eyes were open but the look was vacant.  "OK.  How are you?"

"How do you think I am?  I've had my guts ripped out and they're treating me like I'm crazy."

"Well...dear...you did take an overdose of pills...it could have killed you and the baby."

"I know." It was then that she started to cry. "I'm not crazy, Mother...just upset that Tom is gone. He left me...told me he had made a terrible mistake...I never told him about the baby. Does Anna know?"

"Yes, the baby looks like him and she knew immediately."

"Is she angry with me?"

Ruth couldn't believe the arrogance of that question but she knew that Rachel did not have the sensitivity to realize that.

"I don't know.  You'll have to ask her.  I think that you should be prepared for her to be very angry.  What you did has hurt a lot of people and now Tom is gone.  Your sister is devastated about Tom. Finding out that he fathered a child with you is a monstrous betrayal. I can't say how she will deal with it."

"They keep sending in a psychiatrist and he thinks that I should go to a care facility for a while to work this out. What do you think?"

"I think that would be a good idea. What about the baby?"

"Oh…I don't want the baby. That's why I did it. When I knew that Tom was dead, I didn't want to be in the world without him so I thought if I killed myself and the baby maybe we could all be together in heaven and no one would know."

Ruth heard the words but…could this be her daughter talking? This was the kind of talk that came from crazy people. She knew that it would be important how she responded so she calmly said, "OK. Well Anna and I will take care of the baby for now. You need to go and try to get better."

Ruth kissed Rachel on the forehead and quickly exited the room. She leaned against the wall outside and took a deep breath. What would she tell Anna? Nothing, unless she asks, Ruth decided and headed back to the nursery.

But Anna did not ask. She went about preparing the house for a baby and told the twins that they were going to have a new brother. Rachel was discharged from the hospital and admitted to McLean Hospital, a psychiatric facility in Belmont.

11

They had the Bris on the 8<sup>th</sup> day of the baby's life. Rabbi Cantor came
to the house, Jerry stood in for the Father and the only other people
present were Anna and Ruth.  When asked about the name, Anna
responded that it would be Thaddeus Weiss.    As with Jewish custom,
Anna had taken the first letter of Tom's name and used it for the
baby's name.

Normally a Bris is a joyful occasion celebrating the birth of a son but
this day, the participants were grieving for the child's father as well
as recoiling from the terrible knowledge of the betrayal that had
occurred between twin sisters.

Although Rachel had declared that she did not want the baby,
everyone knew that could change in the blink of an eye. Right now

she was an inpatient at McLean Hospital but she had voluntarily signed herself in so she could sign herself out anytime. That was a fact that weighed heavily on Ruth's mind. Anna was caring for the baby as if he was her own and on the surface, it didn't appear that she even thought about Rachel.

The fact was that the baby was a glorious distraction for Anna and the girls. Losing Tom was tragic and the fact that he died on 9/11 made it even more difficult. Jerry did his best to deflect the reporters and photographers but there was a time when Anna could barely leave the house without someone approaching sticking a microphone in her face or snapping photo.

There seemed to be an insatiable need for details concerning the families of those who died. If they only knew, Ruth thought. The story isn't Anna's bereavement. The story is the new baby. That would be real fodder for the tabloids. She cringed at the thought of the headlines and how the story would spill out into the newspapers.

But as the weeks went on, the publicity died down. There were plenty of families who wanted to bear their souls to the world so they didn't need to cajole Anna. All the people involved in Rachel's hospitalization and Thad's birth kept the sacred trust and eventually, Anna and the children were able to go on rebuilding their life with what was left behind.

When the baby was about a month old, Ruth received a call from McLean. Rachel had signed herself out that morning and left two letters. Ruth was not surprised by the news. She had expected it.

Ruth didn't tell Anna she was going to Belmont. She wanted to see the letters first. So that afternoon, she drove to McLean and picked up the two envelopes. One was addressed to Anna and the other was addressed to Ruth.

She put the one for Anna in her purse and looked at the one labeled Ruth Markowitz. It was Rachel's handwriting. The familiar sense of dread rose up in her as she looked at the writing. She didn't know if she wanted to open it-she had heard it all before but what if this was different? So she tore open the envelope and read,

Dear Mother,
I am going to tell you the truth as I see it and then we will never speak of it again. I have always been jealous of Anna. She always seemed to have everything and I wanted to take something away.

When Tom was working in Washington, I started spending time with him and we had some good times. It was easy for me to see why Anna loved him. I fell deeply in love with him and decided that I would try to get him away from Anna. So one night when we had dinner, we drank a lot of wine and I seduced him. I dressed as much like Anna as I could and tried to act like her. I got him into my bed and I thought I had won until he sobered up and realized what he had done. He was upset and told me it could never happen again.

When I found out that I was pregnant, I called him and called him but he would not return my calls. Then he stopped working on the project in Washington. I kept calling him for a while and then I gave up. Then on 9/11 I got a call from him....he was on the plane and it was going to crash and he just said...."please never tell Anna."

So I am not telling Anna-I am telling you. Anna figured it out herself and I hope she will be able to live with that knowledge. I do not want the baby so I have given Anna the papers relinquishing my parental rights. She should be able to use that to adopt him. I will go back to medical school and continue on with my life but I may not be in touch with you again for a while. You did all that you could. I love you, Rachel

Ruth read the letter three times before she put it back in the envelope. No more tears to shed, she thought.

As she drove back from Belmont, Ruth wondered how Anna would react to this news. With the exception of the few first hours after she heard the news, Anna had been calm and logical in the aftermath of her husband's death. Even the discovery that Tom had fathered Rachel's baby had not disrupted the equanimity of their lives.

The baby had fit into the family seamlessly and seemed to be thriving. Thad was a part of Tom-a legacy that came in an unexpected, tragic way. Anna told the twins that he was going to live with them because their Aunt Rachel wasn't able to take care of him. To three year olds that had just lost their father, it was a simple explanation and a welcome eventuality.

When Ruth got to Anna's house she found her sitting at the kitchen table with a sheaf of papers in front of her.

"Anna...are you OK?"

No response. Ruth walked over and sat down next to her daughter. "Anna?"

Anna turned her head to look at Ruth, "Look...it's the cell phone bill."

Ruth shook her head. "I don't understand .What's wrong?"

"It's the bill for Tom's phone...it ends on 9/11. The last call should be this number but it isn't...it's Rachel's number. She was the last person to hear his voice. He was my husband and I should have been the last one to hear his voice. When will this end?"

"Anna….Rachel signed herself out of McLean and she left two letters. One was addressed to me and the other is for you."

"Tear it up…I never want to speak of her again. She stole a part of my husband and I can't forgive that."

"I can't do that because I know what's in the envelope. She has signed away her rights to Thad and wants you to adopt him."

Anna looked stunned. "What?"

"She doesn't want the baby. She told me what happened and it isn't what you think."

"How could it not be what I think…she had my husband's? baby?"

"I know. Of course, it is partly Tom's fault but he didn't know about the baby…it happened once when she tricked him. He never had anything to do with her after that and she didn't have a chance to tell him about the baby. That's the reason he switched projects…so that he wouldn't be in the Washington area."

"And the change in projects is what put him on that plane so she killed him and n o w she expects me to mother her love child."

The harshness of the words was shocking but, Ruth thought, it was close to the truth.

"I know and you will…you have enough room in your heart for Thad…no matter how he came into your life."

Anna looked at her Mother with pleading eyes and said, "Yes....I do.. Show me the letter."

Ruth pulled the envelope from her purse and Anna opened it. It was, as Rachel said, paperwork relinquishing Rachel's parental rights. It was all legal and professional. There was nothing personal but that was no surprise. Rachel showed some remorse in her letter to Ruth but she would not do the same for Anna. That would be a sign of weakness and Rachel didn't have the sensitivity to show that to her sister.

Anna read the letter twice and then she shook her head and said, "She never apologizes. The least she could do is tell me that she is sorry. Tom did."

Ruth thought for a moment and said, "Anna...she doesn't know how to do that. You know that."

"I know. It just continues to amaze me that she is so insensitive and cold. I'll see the lawyer tomorrow and get the ball rolling."

Before she could say more, the clear sound of a baby's cry punctuated the air. Anna stood up and as she walked out of the kitchen she said, "I'll just go get my son."

## 12

On the same day that the judge made the ruling that legally declared Tom Weiss dead, he also finalized the adoption of Thaddeus Weiss-alpha and omega-the beginning and the end. And the healing went on.

Anna hired an au pair to care for the children while she went back to teaching. The twins were enrolled in a preschool program at the Jewish Community Center and Thad went to infant activity classes with the au pair. From the outside, it had all the trappings of a typical family except... there was no father or husband.

There was the inevitable notoriety. Being a 9/11 widow marked her and Anna could feel the eyes on her when she was at the supermarket.

It seemed that everyone tried to be a little nicer than usual. Even the dreaded lady at the deli counter smiled at her and packaged her cold cuts with a little more care than usual. The woman had adored Tom and had disliked it when Anna showed up without him. Anna's punishment for not shopping with Tom had always been sliced cheese that had been smashed together and deli meat that was shredded to the consistency of cat food. Now the woman was being kindly and Anna found it unnerving.

Were they all waiting for her to throw a nutty in the middle of the produce department? Would Tom's love of broccoli make her have a hysterical episode?

Admittedly, at first, she did have anxious moments at the market. She would automatically reach for Oreos and then remember that they were Tom's favorite. She disapproved of the cookies being available for the girls so, Tom would hide the package in their bedroom and feast on them at night after the girls were sleeping.

But it wasn't only the shopping. It was the house and how Tom's absence echoed in every room.

On Friday night when it was time to light Sabbath candles she ached to hear Tom bless the children and do the Kiddush for the wine and challah. She would sit alone on Friday night and that was when she would allow herself to remember. It became a Sabbath ritual and as the weeks and months went by, the memories became less raw and painful and she could remember the joy and love.

But the real elephant in the room was Thad. No one asked but there were questioning stares. Where did that baby come from? Anna knew that there were rumors but she also knew that people were going to talk. Her Grandmother had always said..."Let them talk about me. That means they're leaving someone else alone." So that was Anna's philosophy. She held her head high and moved forward with dignity.

Requests for interviews poured in via the mail, telephone, computer and some really cheeky reporters who came to the door. The mail contained endless paperwork and Jerry took care of that for her. Since that terrible day Anna had gained a new appreciation for Jerry and how he protected Ruth and her family.

While she was able to make the ordinary day to day decisions, she had no idea what to do about the big decisions. Should she join in the lawsuits? What about the victim's fund? Should she allow an interview? Would they ever go away?

And then one day Jerry came to her with a small envelope. She had seen the return address and tossed it in the basket of mail for Jerry to handle. He asked her to sit down and told her that she needed to look at what was in the envelope.

Anna perched on the edge of the chair and took the small, padded envelope from Jerry. Inside she found a letter but she gasped when she saw that the envelope contained the remains of Tom's wallet.

She had been asked to provide material for a DNA sample and photos of Tom but she never thought she would receive any of his personal effects. She had seen the plane crash and the building burst into flames so she thought that there would probably be no physical remains but here it was. Sealed in an evidence envelope was the brown leather wallet she had given him for Father's Day. She opened the plastic envelope and reached in to touch the wallet. It was charred and the leather had absorbed a terrible odor that was a combination of jet fuel, smoke and death.

Nothing had prepared her for this moment and she felt her head start to spin. Jerry knelt down next to her and said, "Honey, it's a shock. Let's put it away until later."

Anna handed the bag to Jerry and said, "I don't want the girls to see it. They'll be home soon."

Jerry left the room with the bag and a few minutes later he returned with two glasses of cognac. "I put it in your closet. Here drink this."

They sat together sipping the cognac and Anna started to feel the shock recede. "Thank you. I just didn't expect to receive anything. I just assumed it was all vaporized."

"I know but they have been sifting through the rubble and They do find personal effects. You'll be able to look at it after a while. Just get used to the fact that it is here and then you'll know when the time is right."

So the envelope loomed in her mind and she mulled it over and over in her mind. Finally she decided that it was something to share with the girls. Father's Day was coming up and they would look at it then.

The weather that day was gloomy which matched the mood in their house. Thad was fussy and the girls seemed subdued. They didn't say anything but Anna knew that they had heard a lot about Father's Day at school.

After a favorite breakfast of waffles and strawberries, Anna told the girls that she had something important to show them.

They sat at the table and Anna brought out the envelope. The girls looked at her with curiosity and fear.

"A few weeks ago I received this in the mail. It belonged to Daddy so I thought that we would look at it together."

"It belonged to Daddy?" asked Hannah. "Where has it been?"

"Well some very nice people have been going through all of the rubble and someone found this. It's Daddy's wallet."

Anna placed the wallet in front of the girls and said, "Go ahead...it's OK to touch it."

Slowly and tentatively the little hands reached out and gently touched the scorched leather. As quickly as the hands went out, they went back again and Miriam whispered, " It's been burned. Did Daddy burn?"

Anna quickly tried to deflect the question. She didn't want to dwell on the burn marks and hoped that the girls' curiosity was momentary. "Daddy always left his wallet in his briefcase when he travelled. Let's look inside."

Anna gently opened the wallet and found that the interior was mostly undamaged. Tom's driver's license and credit cards were in the usual slots. Anna pulled out the driver's license and felt a lump rise in her throat when she saw that the expiration date was three years away.

Reaching into one of the inside pockets, Anna pulled out some business cards and then she found the photos. She spread them out on the table and the girl's gaped at the images.

There was a photo of Anna holding the twins for the first time, a photo of the twins' first birthday party and a recent family photo. They were well worn and slightly singed around the edges. Anna's throat closed up as she looked at the pictures. She had never known that Tom carried them with him.

Hannah reached out and touched the photos reverently. "We were with him all the time."

"Yes. Your Daddy carried us with him everywhere."

So their family unit sat at the table and pored over the Contents of the wallet but the girls' eyes rarely left the photos.

After they had gone through everything twice, Anna said, "Let's put this away for now. I think that Thad would like to go to the park. What do you think?"

At the mention of the park, the girls brightened and they raced down the hallway to finish dressing.

Anna watched them retreat from the room and she marveled at the resilience of youth. These little girls had suffered a devastating loss but they moved on.

Whether or not to show them the wallet had been a hard decision. There had been so many situations where she had needed to shield the girls but she knew that they had thoughts that were difficult to form into questions.

Neither of the girls spoke of their loss in anything but a peripheral way. They would speak of family outings with Daddy or point to a storybook that Daddy had liked to read.

Anna had hired a therapist who specialized in grief counseling for children. The therapist had assured Anna that the twins were responding appropriately and advised Anna to try to keep their family life as normal as possible. So far it seemed to be working and Thad was a welcome distraction. The girls adored their baby brother and never seemed concerned about how and why he had become a member of their family.

## 13

As the first anniversary of the event approached, there was renewed interest in Anna's family. Reporters called and wanted to know how the family was coping but Anna stuck to her no interview posture until the organizers of the one year observance called. They wanted to know if the twins would read Tom's name. Anna thought they were too young but the efficient young woman assured her that there would be other young children involved-some younger than the twins.

So one night after dinner, Anna sat down with the girls and they discussed whether the girls would participate in the remembrance event. There were questions. Practical questions-where would they go if they needed a bathroom? Logistical questions-where would they stand and could they reach the microphone? Security questions-where would Anna be standing? Never once did they seem reluctant and when Anna was able to give them a reasonable response to their questions, they seemed reassured.

Anna wanted to make sure that they understood that there would be a lot of people and cameras so she said, "There'll be a lot of people there. Will that make you afraid?"

Miriam looked solemnly at Anna and asked, "Will there be other little girls who lost their Daddy?"

"Yes, there will be many people who lost people they loved."

It was Hannah's turn, "Will it make everyone feels better if we are brave and read our Daddy's name?"

Anna fought back tears and said, "It will and it will make me proud."

"Will Daddy be able to hear us?" whispered Miriam.

The innocence of the question was heartbreaking but Anna reached out to her daughter and said, "Yes, Daddy will be listening and he will be so proud of his brave little girls."

And that was how they made the decision to go to New York for the first anniversary remembrance. There were many coordinators and endless instructions but when the time came, the girls' held hands as they approached the microphone and said, "Our Daddy, Thomas Weiss."

Anna's heart was ready to burst with a mixture of sadness and pride. Thad was snuggled in her arms and she squeezed him tightly as she looked at the sky and wondered if Tom could see them.
.
The air in that area of New York was full of souls. Anna found it stifling but she knew one of those souls was Tom. She kept reminding herself of that as she watched other survivors trying to comfort each other.

Everyone had different reasons for being there. Some were saying goodbye and others seemed to be seeking answers. Anna was there for forgiveness. She needed to be able to forgive Tom and when she was able to do that she would be able to forgive her sister.

The 9/11 grief was different in Boston. Since the planes had taken off from Logan, there were many survivors but because of the smoldering crater in New York, the world's focus rested there.

Not that Anna wanted the focus on her. She still had real ambivalence about that day. It was an itch that she swore to never scratch. Some days the urge was overwhelming but she busied herself with the mundane details of raising her family and tried to ignore the emotions that were always so close to the surface.

This was her first trip to Ground Zero. Eventually she had been able to watch the news again. The twins had started to have questions so she had told them a version of the story of 9/11. They never questioned her about Thad who was one year old today. He was walking and trying to talk but most of the time it was too garbled to be understood. He was a charming little boy who laughed easily and adored his older sisters. Anna knew that she couldn't love him more if she had given birth to him herself.

Rachel had been in touch with Ruth only once and had never asked about Thad. When Tom's name rang out on the loud speakers, Anna had the strangest feeling that Rachel was there but in the throng of people, it would be impossible to distinguish one person from another. She was sure she was imagining it.

Once they were back in Boston, Anna decided that it was time to deal with her residual grief. There were groups for 9/11 survivors but she avoided being in a group where everyone was focusing on their loved one dying from a terrorist attack. She found a bereavement group through the Jewish Federation and with enormous trepidation; she went to her first meeting.

To her surprise, it wasn't morbid or sad. Yes, people cried but there was an aura of hopefulness in the group and that was an emotion she latched onto for dear life. And as the weeks went by, she started to share-not the details of the infidelity but the details of her grief and slowly the weight she had been carrying lessened.

After two months, she started to understand that people had real issues about losing a spouse. It wasn't all sweetness and light. There was survivor's guilt but there was also anger and feelings of abandonment. The most difficult were those who had a spiritual crisis and could not accept the seeming randomness of death. Why one person and not another? Why a good person as opposed to an evil person? Why a child and not an elderly person?

One night, Anna was walking to her car when she heard a voice behind her.

"Anna, can I talk to you for a minute?"

She turned around to see Ryan, a young widower whose wife had died in childbirth. He was tall and painfully thin but as the weeks went by; his face had started to soften as he shared his story with the group.

She smiled and said, "Sure."

Ryan seemed embarrassed and he started stammering a little when he said, "Well...I was just wondering ...well...would you like to go have a cup of coffee?"

Anna looked at this serious, kind looking man and before she knew it, she blurted out, "Well...yes. That would be nice."

And that was the start of what would turn into a deep love and commitment. It took time and patience but Ryan and Anna found that they had enough room in their hearts to love each other.

## 14

Ryan's wife, Barbara, had died giving birth of their daughter, Faith. There had been no complications in the pregnancy but she had suffered a stroke during the delivery and was dead before she ever saw her baby.

As he buried Barbara, the woman he had loved since high school, Ryan knew that he needed to reach out to his family for help with the baby. It was difficult to accept that he was now a single father and the responsibility of parenthood coupled with the grief of losing his spouse had sent him reeling into serious depression.

With an intervention by his Mother, he began seeing a therapist. Gradually he came to accept his loss and unravel the complex knot of feelings towards his daughter. Faith was not directly responsible for her Mother's death but there was an undeniable connection. The date of Faith's birth was the date of her Mother's death.

Now two years later, Ryan was finally reaching out socially. He had listened to Anna's story and felt drawn to her. It had taken him weeks to get up the courage to ask her to have coffee but after that, it all seemed to fall into place.

One evening as they took a quiet moment for a glass of wine, Anna told him the whole story. Not the sanitized version she told most people but everything. He listened carefully and when she was finished, he said, "So Thad's birth date is the date of his father's death; just like Faith."

"Yes. They have that in common."

"Well, I think they should have more in common. Will you marry me?"

Anna's first thought was that although she hadn't expected him to propose so soon; it had been inevitable. They had been on the path to marriage ever since that fateful night when Ryan got up the courage to ask her out for coffee.

It wasn't the same love as they had for the spouses they had lost but the difference made it special and pure. They both knew it was a blessing and they took special care to nourish and protect their love.

On 9/11/03, Ryan Cohen and Anna Weiss were married by Rabbi Cantor. They made their chuppah from Tom's prayer shawl and scarves that had belonged to Ryan's wife, Barbara. Miriam, Hannah, Thad and Faith read vows to each other and the family before lighting candles of unity.

Everyone said it was touching and unique but the new Weiss- Cohen family knew it was more than that. It was the beginning of a new life where they would honor the past and rejoice in the future but most of all they would love each other in the present.

On their first anniversary Anna told Ryan that she was expecting a baby. It was a rare night out at a favorite neighborhood restaurant and Anna was dismayed as she watched the color drained from Ryan's face.

She had known that it would a shock but now she was wondering if he would require medical attention.

"Ryan? Are you OK?"

Ryan stared at her with a look of incredulity mixed with a hint of happiness. "I'm OK. I'm surprised and I just had a terrible rush of emotion about Barbara."

Anna reached out for her husband's hand and said, "I know. It's OK. When I got the results I remembered giving Tom the news about the twins. It's natural that we should have memories. We just need to remember that this is different...we are different."

Ryan grasped her hand and nodded his head. It wasn't necessary for him to speak, his touch made up for the lack of words.

As Anna's belly grew and the doctor pronounced her to be in excellent health, Ryan allowed himself to relax. The doctor knew the history with Ryan's first wife so he was careful in discussing the labor and delivery with Ryan.

But when Anna's labor started, Ryan alternated between being a dutiful husband and labor coach and out and out terror. The labor team knew about his past experience and they watched over him carefully to make sure that he was able to handle the anxiety. There were two patients that night- Anna and her terrified husband.

But then Benjamin Michael Weiss-Cohen was born. Ryan had locked his hand on Anna's and had to be coaxed away to cut the cord and hold his son. He did it all but his eyes never left Anna who was tired and spent but very much alive.

## 15

With five children in the house, life was hectic but they always remembered to count the blessings in their lives. Every year on 9/11, Thad received a birthday card from his Aunt Rachel but there was never any other type of communication.

Since 9/11 was Thad's birthday as well as their wedding anniversary they chose to commemorate the date with family outings. It was a day of remembrance for them but also a day of celebration. Every year there was a family vote and the majority ruled in picking a destination. Several times when the day fell on a weekend, they had gone down to Cape Cod for a few days.

Each year, Anna asked the girls if they wanted to go to New York but they never seemed to be interested and always voted for a different type of family outing.

In the summer of 2011, Hannah and Miriam came to their Mother. As usual, Hannah was the spokesperson.

"It's going to be the 10th anniversary of the 9/11 attacks and there is going to be a memorial with all the names. We would like to go see our Daddy's name."

Until know they had only seen their Daddy's name on the Yahrzeit board at temple. They knew all about that remembrance of the dead but they had only participated in the official 9/11 remembrance that one time in 2002. They were almost too young to remember. This was the first time they had asked to go to New York and Anna knew that, after ten years, it was time.

"OK. We'll go.

"We heard that there are a lot of people and they have to limit the number of people per family. So we should just take Thad and Granny."

"Who said?"

"The woman on the TV. We heard her talking about it and decided to ask you."

"OK. I'll call and make the arrangements."

So on 9/11/11 Anna followed her Mother and children down into the memorial. It was a solemn, serious procession of people who had suffered terrible losses. It was remarkably quiet and peaceful within the memorial as people walked along to find the name of their loved one.

Many people carried flowers and photos. The girls had brought their Bat Mitzvah photos and Anna had brought a red carnation. Her heart beat quickly in anticipation of how it would feel to see Tom's name etched in the memorial. The girls and Thad marched forward and Ruth helped them find Tom's name.

Anna stepped back and watched the girls as they slowly approached the name. Their hands reached out and they ran fingers over the letters. Anna could see that their lips were moving but she could not hear what they said. After a moment, they knelt down and kissed the name.

And then much to Anna's surprise, they took Thad's hand and lead him over to the name. Words were whispered into his ears and he reached out and gently touched the letters.

Then it was Anna's turn. She walked over and looked down at the name. Thomas Weiss-her husband and first love. For the first time in years, she was overwhelmed with the remembrance of their love. And it surprised her that she did not feel anger. For years, the betrayal had marked her memories but it wasn't there anymore.

The 9/11 attacks had taken Tom out of the equation of the betrayal. He never knew he had conceived a child with Rachel. When Tom said he was sorry, he had meant that he was sorry about being with Rachel. He had died without knowing about the baby. Anna could speculate about what would have happened when the truth of the baby was revealed. Thad was the image of Tom so there would have been no denying the paternity.

But it was all speculation. Anna liked to think that she would have been able to forgive but there was always Thad. If Tom had not died, what would have happened to the child?

Rachel was spectacularly unfit to handle motherhood but would she have tried? The child would have been a permanent link between Rachel and Tom. Of course, there would have been the obvious financial obligations but Anna knew Tom well enough to know that he would never have turned his back on his own child. But fate had stepped in and Thad had become Anna's son.

When Anna stepped up to Tom's name, she felt her heart open and she murmured, "Hello Tom. Aren't the girls beautiful? And that was your son but I think you already knew that. Rachel gave him to me. You would love him. I'm married to a wonderful man named Ryan. We have a son and our blended family has five children so we are busy. It's a good family and everyone is happy. I will always make sure that the girls' remember you just as I will always remember you as my husband. I love you and carry you in my heart always." Anna knelt down and kissed the name and then turned back to her family. Ruth spent a brief moment in front of the name and then they moved on. No one ever discussed what they said but from that day on, the ghost of Tom seemed to have been released.

Many people called it closure but Anna hated that word. They had closed nothing. Tom would always be a part of the fabric of their life but his memory no longer held fear. Anna knew that her emotions about Tom had been settled and she had peace. Now she needed to go on with the parts of her life that were still in the present.

## 16

Anna knew that Rachel was practicing medicine in Chicago. Ruth had told her that.

The last words between the sisters were when Rachel had barged into Anna's bedroom and started burrowing into Tom's closet. Rachel had been rambling incoherently and Anna had pleaded with her to leave the room. Since then the only communication had been when Rachel sent Anna the paperwork to adopt Thad.

Anna had spent most of her life trying to separate herself from her twin. Being estranged from Rachel felt familiar but as Anna's twins grew she watched their relationship and wondered what it would be like to have a twin sister who is your best friend.

Anna and Rachel had never been friends. They had never even shared the same friends. It was a mutual feeling and Anna had never felt that she needed to nurture a relationship with Rachel.

After Anna married Tom and became a mother, she had her own family and did not feel the need to extend herself to her sister. What good would it have done? Rachel seemed to be equally uninterested in her twin sister so there was a mutual neglect of their relationship

Tom had not mentioned that he had been in contact with Rachel. If he had, Anna would have told her that it would lead to heartache but Tom had never accepted that Rachel was anything other than quirky and unpredictable.

Certainly neither of them would have ever imagined anything like what actually happened. How could they?

Anna supposed that her lack of involvement in the family, gave Rachel a sort of mystique. No wonder Tom was curious about his sister-in-law.

When Thad was twelve, they enrolled him in classes for his Bar Mitzvah. He had grown into a tall, lanky young man who was so like Tom it was unnerving. Ryan had been the only Father he ever knew and Thad never asked any questions about his biological father. He knew that Rachel had given birth to him and that his father had died but he never asked Anna any other questions.

There were lots of family videos of the twins when Tom was alive and when they watched, no one mentioned that Thad looked a lot like the twins' Daddy. It was such a non-issue that Anna and Ryan felt it was best to leave it at that unless they were asked a direct question.

Thad flew through Hebrew school and seemed to enjoy studying his Torah section with the young assistant Rabbi. Rabbi James had suggested that Thad write part of the service so they met regularly planning the order of the service and the music.

Anna marveled at the interest Thad showed in the process. The twins had used the standard liturgy and their service had incorporated the whole family. Anna still remembered how proud she had been as her girls lead the service. She had wished that Tom could have been there to see the beautiful, graceful young women his little girls had become.

Part of the process was choosing a Bar Mitzvah Project. His sisters had done a fund raising project to develop a program for grieving children. After their own experience of grieving as three year olds, it was natural for them to want to give back to other children who suffered the loss of a parent. Ryan and Anna had been pleasantly surprised by the project and it had been such a spectacular success that the local school district had incorporated it into their family support system.

Thad researched projects but did not seem interested in any of the typical choices-food pantry, animal shelter or the hospital. After several weeks of internet research and books checked out of the library, Thad came to them and said that he had made his big decision.

He was very serious when he explained, "I walk outside and every yard has soccer balls and basketball hoops. We have so much that we forget to even take care of all of it. We leave our bicycles and scooters lying out on the lawn. There are kids who don't even have one soccer ball. I have three. I could ask my friends to donate their extra stuff. I talked to Rabbi James about it and we called the director of a youth center in Dorchester. My school principal is going to let me make an announcement requesting donations. He'll let us use the gym for storage and then I'll ask some people to help me deliver the stuff. What do you think?"

Anna was speechless. Where did this luminous young man get his generous nature? Of course, she knew...but it was always surprising when she saw Tom's spirit shining through his son.

Thad went from door to door in the neighborhood cajoling kids to donate their extra or outgrown sports equipment. An announcement was posted at the Jewish Community Center and before they knew it, they had boxes and boxes of donated sports gear.

It took three vans to deliver the boxes to Dorchester. Ryan organized a pizza party so that Thad and some of his friends could meet the kids that use the youth center.

At first it was a bit like a scene out of "West Side Story" but after the boxes were opened, the basketballs started flying around the room. In a matter of minutes, the group had organized a pickup game. Soon the gym was filled with laughter and playful banter. By the time they left the center, Thad was aglow with excitement over his new friends.

As the got on the highway to head back to Brookline, Thad looked at Ryan and said, "That was the most fun I have had in a long time."

"I'm glad. Your mother and I are very proud of you."

"I know. Do you think my real Dad would be proud too?" Ryan's

mind went blank as he gripped the steering wheel and tried to not drive over a curb. Wham...he thought...this is like a Josh Beckett fast ball whistling past you.

The question and it came while he was at bat. How he answered was crucial but then he remembered what his wife always said, Sometimes a question is just a question. They just want to know the time so you don't need to tell them how to make a watch. So he looked at his son and said, "Yes I do Thad...very proud indeed."

And that was it. Within a few minutes they were chatting about the Red Sox and Thad's latest soccer game.

## 17

Later that evening, Ryan and Anna were cuddled up on the sofa, having a private moment. The twins and Faith had gone to a slumber party which meant that they would return the next day feeling cranky from too little slumber and too much party.

Dealing with three teenage girls on the day after a slumber party was always a challenge so Anna and Ryan had stolen away to the living room for a few minutes of quiet time. From the sound of it, the boys were playing some sort of video game in the den and the house seemed very peaceful.

Anna was anxious to hear details of the visit to Dorchester. When she asked Thad he had just said that it was fun. Anna knew enough about her son to know that there wouldn't be further details so she was relying on her husband to elaborate.

Ryan told her everything and they laughed over the antics of the group of boys and the amount of pizza they consumed. Then Ryan decided he must tell Anna about Thad's question.

"I told Thad that we were very proud of him and he asked me if I thought his real Dad would be proud of him?"

Anna was shocked. It was the question. Thad had never

asked anything remotely like that.  "What did you say?"

"Well...I went by your credo that sometimes a question is just a question and went for the short answer. I told him yes, I thought he would be very proud indeed."

"And what did Thad say?"

"Nothing. Before I knew it were talking about the Red Sox and the moment was gone."

"Do you think I should tell him?"

"That's up to you, Anna."

"Oh come on Ryan....you must have an opinion."

Ryan smiled at his wife and said, "I think sometimes a question is just a question."

Anna snuggled up to her husband and said, "So do I."

## 18

The following Wednesday morning, Anna was in her kitchen cleaning up the breakfast dishes when the doorbell rang. She didn't have a class until the afternoon so she was being leisurely in puttering around the quiet house. From the window she could see the big brown UPS truck and she thought it must be something that Ryan had ordered.

After retrieving the package, she saw her name written in handwriting she had not seen in over fifteen years.
She placed the package on the counter and picked up the telephone to call her mother.

When Ruth answered, she said, "Hi. Mom. I've just received a package from Rachel. Can you come over?"

"How do you know it's from Rachel?"

"I recognized the handwriting. I haven't opened it. I'm afraid of what's inside."

"I'll be right over."

Ruth lived only a few minutes away but the time passed slowly for Anna. The package sat on the counter and Anna tried to walk around the edge of the kitchen to avoid being too close to it. She knew it was probably ridiculous but she had a really bad feeling about the package.

When her Mother's car drew into the driveway she raced to the door to greet her.

"It's in the kitchen."

Ruth looked at her daughter. Anna's face was pale and her eyes were filled with fear. "Anna, you look like you seen a ghost."

Anna just stared at her mother and then the tears started to spill down her cheeks. "She is a ghost. Whatever is in that box will hurt my family."

Ruth reached out and hugged her daughter. "Honey, we don't know that."

"Oh yes I do. What if she wants Thad back? "

"Well then you would receive a letter. She wouldn't send a box for that. Now don't jump to conclusions. It's been thirteen years. Do you want me to open it?"

"Yes."

So Ruth found scissors and carefully opened the box. Cradled inside bubble wrap was a photo album. She lifted it from the box and looked to see if there was a card or letter but there was none.

Ruth handed the album to Anna and said, "Open it. I think it will tell you a story."

Anna poured herself a cup of coffee and sat down at the table. Ruth had placed the album in front of her but she could not bring herself to touch it.

Ruth sat down next to her and said, "Let's look at it together...OK?"

Ruth opened the cover and on the first page was a photo of Rachel and Anna when they were Bat Mitzvah. They had shared a service but looking at the photo, you could see the chasm between the two girls.

Anna was dressed in a navy blue suit, a white cashmere sweater and a string of pearls. She looked grown up and sophisticated. The suit had been purchased at Bonwit Teller during a special shopping trip with Ruth. After they left the store with the suit, they had gone to tea at the Ritz before going across the street to see the Make Way for Ducklings statues in the Boston Public Garden. It was a special childhood memory for Anna because it had no smear by Rachel. There were not many memories that were not covered with Rachel.

Of course, Rachel had been offered the chance to shop with them at Bonwit Teller and she had scoffed at the mere suggestion of such a venture. Rachel had said that she wouldn't be caught dead in anything purchased on Newbury Street. She had sneered at Ruth telling her that she was boring and then laughed at Anna for wanting to wear a boring, uptight suit. How well Anna remembered that exchange. She could still recall how her cheeks had burned with embarrassment at her sister's words.

In the photo, Rachel was dressed in a black top over a short plaid skirt. The photo didn't show their feet but Anna remembered that Rachel had worn black leather boots.

Their Father had been enlisted to take Rachel shopping in Harvard Square and they had come home with the preposterous outfit. Anna remembered that her father had looked harassed and ashamed when Rachel strutted around the house in her new finery. No one ever mentioned the shopping trip again but after that, Rachel was allowed to go shopping alone.

Why include this photo? Their Bat Mitzvah was about the last act of family compliance for Rachel and Anna had always suspected that their father had bribed her to do it.

"How much did Dad pay Rachel to go through with the Bat Mitzvah?"

Ruth drew in a breath and then chuckled, "I don't know but I know they had some sort of deal. Your father didn't tell me details because he knew I wouldn't approve. How did you know?"

"Well...Rachel wasn't much for doing the right thing and it was hard work studying for that Bat Mitzvah. She was doing it for a reason and not just to please you...she never did anything that didn't benefit her in some way."

Ruth hated to hear such cynicism from Anna but she knew that her daughter had every reason in the world to resent her sister. Anna had spent her life in the background while the family's attention was on Rachel and whatever drama she was experiencing.

It had been difficult to try to keep some semblance of family life and it often left Ruth with a choice between her daughters. Anna had been lower maintenance and had tended to stay behind the scenes while Rachel stole the limelight. If only….thought Ruth….if only I had been able to make her understand.

"Shall I go on?"

Anna was still staring at the first photo and bracing herself for what would be on the next page.

Ruth turned the page and what came next was a photo taken in front of Camden Yards in Baltimore. Anna looked at the page and felt a cold tremor of fear grip her body. She could feel the gorge rising in her throat as she raced down the hallway to the bathroom.

She bent over the toilet as she emptied her stomach and suddenly she had a flash back to that terrible day when Tom died. All the energy had been drained from her body and she was too weak to get up from the floor.

Was this how Tom had felt on the plane when he knew he was going to die? This was a question that had always been under the surface. One of the places she did not allow herself to go. What had he thought as the plane crashed?

The scene was familiar, Anna remembered that horrible day and sitting on the tile floor of her bathroom wishing she could just fall away into oblivion. Now she was, once again, on the floor of a bathroom feeling overwhelmed by raw, fierce emotions.

Ruth watched Anna retreat from the room and sat motionless at the table. What did this picture mean? She peered closely at the photo and saw that it was Tom with his arm around a woman that looked like Anna. It took a moment but then in a terrible flash, Ruth realized that it wasn't Anna. It was Rachel pretending to be Anna.

Ruth knocked on the bathroom door which was partially ajar. "Anna...are you O K . " Ruth knelt down on the floor and put her arms around her daughter.

There was nothing to say. This was the pent up emotion and heartache that had built up over thirteen years. Now it was coming out of every pore of Anna's body.

Ruth held her daughter as she shook and wailed. When the shaking stopped, Anna gulped and said, "I've never been to Camden Yards."

"I know, honey, I know."

It's so cruel that she should send me that picture."

Ruth thought about it for a minute and said, "Maybe not so

cruel. I think she is trying to tell you a story. I know that it is heartbreaking for you but it may be a message from your sister."

Anna was spent. She clung to her mother for support as she got up from the floor. Ruth tenderly washed Anna's face and said, "Let's look at the rest and try to see what she is saying."

When they got back to the kitchen, Ruth automatically filled the kettle to make tea. Anna said, "Mom, why do people always make tea when something terrible happens?"

"I don't know. Do you want me to turn the kettle off?"

"No. I just wondered. The day Tom died, you made me tea and I remember thinking that you didn't know what else to do so you made tea. It's not a criticism. It's an observation."

"I know honey. That was such a terrible day and I couldn't do anything to make it go away so I did what I knew I could do which was make tea. That's what Mothers do."

Anna laughed and Ruth could see that some of the color was coming back into her cheeks. "Let's keep looking."

The next pages were a series of photos of Thad. But how?

"She wasn't here...where did these pictures come from?"

Ruth had no explanation. She turned to the last page and found a photo of Anna and Thad at the first 9/11 ceremony. The last photo was Tom's name on the memorial.

Anna's hands were shaking as she closed the book. "What does this mean?"

Ruth shook her head and then said, "I'm not sure but I think it is Rachel's way of reaching out to you."

Anna's eyes flashed and he voice was cold and sharp as she said,

"Or to show me that she can get near to my son any time she wants. You know...I knew that first 9/11 that she was there. I could feel it and I have felt her presence around me when I am with Thad. Mom, it's creepy like something horrible is going to happen. It could be right out of a Stephen King novel where the psycho is right behind you but you don't know it."

Ruth could understand Anna's anger. The fact that Rachel had been lurking around Thad was unsettling. Although Rachel had relinquished her parental rights, Ruth suspected tha Anna always dreaded the day when her twin would go through one of her mercurial moods and show up on Anna's doorstep to claim her son. In Anna's mind, the photo album was a threat to her family and it was understandable that she was in mother bear mode.

Ruth sat helplessly as Anna trembled with anger and fright. She knew that Rachel was troubled but she didn't think that her daughter was capable of inflicting any physical harm. But going back to the night of Thad's birth, it did make you wonder. Rachel had been delusional and had tried to kill herself and the baby thinking that they could be together with Tom in heaven. Ruth had always tried to squelch that memory. She had never shown anyone the contents of Rachel's letter-not even Jerry. The thought that Rachel meant any harm to Anna and her family was too monstrous. Ruth could not allow herself to even consider the possibility.

"I still think that she is trying to send you a message. She's reaching out by showing you a picture of what was probably the last family time you two shared. She chose a picture of her with Tom to show you that she had tried so hard to look like you. She watched Thad grow and then showed you in a typical mother/child posture. I think she is showing you what a good life you have. She's showing you your son. They're pictures for a proud mother. She wants to show you that she has seen Thad grow and she knows that she made the right decision. I think it is her way of apologizing."

Anna looked at the album and opened it to the first page. She touched the photo of her with Rachel and she said, "We were so young. The same age as Thad is now. I look at my twins and I know I missed so much about having a sister. They are so close and Rachel and I were never more than occupants of the same house. Did you ever wonder why?"

Ruth frowned and said, "Of course I did. It broke my heart that you weren't close but after a while I had to stop caring about that and try to do my best with each of you as individuals. I failed miserably with Rachel but I hope I was able to give you some of the mothering you needed."

"You did the best you could. I learned to understand that you loved us both. Even though Rachel was rebellious and antisocial, she is your daughter and you love her. That's what a mother does.

## 19

Ruth rarely talked to Anna about her childhood. It was always so deeply fraught with Rachel episodes and Ruth was afraid to hear what Anna thought about her upbringing. So they had always talked about it in the most general terms.

Anna touched the picture again and said, "Do you remember when we went to Bonwit Teller to buy that suit and Dad ended up in Harvard Square with Rachel. That must have been so awful for him but he did it. He was a good man."

"Yes, your father was a good man but he had a blind spot when it came to Rachel. In his defense, he wasn't always a witness to the Rachel tantrums and verbal assaults. She served those up when she was out of his earshot or when he was not at home. She knew exactly how to manipulate him and he never saw her flip side. She always showed him Side A and saved Side B for us. I know he eventually woke up about Rachel but by then she was lost to us. It was always a difficult part of our marriage. At first I used to talk to him about it but he always had excuses. It was much later that he finally accepted that she was out of control. It was too much for him when he realized how it had hurt you but he was too proud to talk to you about it. When he was dying he finally talked about it and told me how sorry he was that he had not believed me. It was a bittersweet moment because it was only when I was about to lose him that I finally got vindication."

"I never knew that."

"Honey, that was private between me and my husband. I just couldn't talk about it then. After he died and Rachel showed up from California I remember thinking that without her father she would lose all self-control at his funeral but…she didn't. Her behavior was exemplary but I think that was just a fluke. She was probably taking her meds."

Anna gasped. "Her meds?"

"Yes, her meds. Anna, your sister has been on and off meds since she was sixteen years old. She was diagnosed as a borderline personality but that was c h a n g e d to bipolar."

"Why didn't anyone tell me?"

"Because I thought that your sister deserved privacy and I didn't want to frighten you. She begged me to not tell your father so I didn't until years later when she had a crisis and it became an issue. That was a mistake…I know that now but I felt that I needed to protect her."

Anna could see the pain in her mother's eyes. As a mother herself, she couldn't imagine having to make the decisions that her mother made over Rachel. "You did what you thought was best. It's all a mother can do."

I'm glad that your father didn't live to see what happened with Tom. I don't think he would have been able to handle it."

"I know, Mom. It's only since I have been married and had five children in the house that I see how hard it was for you. My kids are normal and well behaved but there are days when one of them will be grumpy and it passes through the family like a virus. Those are the days when I wonder how I would handle a child who behaved like Rachel. I suppose I shouldn't speak too soon, the twins are just sixteen and we have some teenage years to come."

"They will be fine. You have done a spectacular job as a mother and you have chosen well in men. Tom was a good man who made a terrible mistake and fate denied him the chance to atone. Ryan is a wonderful man and you have worked together to develop a wonderful blended family. Does Thad ever say anything about his father?"

"Funny that you should ask that. Ryan was in the car with him coming back from Dorchester after they delivered all that sports equipment and he told Thad that he was very proud of him. Then Thad asked Ryan if he thought his real Dad would be proud of him as well."

"Oh poor Ryan...the question...what did he say?"

Anna giggled and said, "Well he used my advice that with kids, sometimes a question is just a question so you give them a direct answer and move on. So he said that he thought his real Dad would be very proud and then they next thing he knew they knew they were talking about the Red Sox."

"But it wasn't an idle question. You do know that don't you?"

Anna sighed and said, "Yes….I know that but I just don't know where to begin. It's a complicated story. The girls took it very well but I don't know about Thad. "

"When did you tell the girls?"

"They started to notice the similarity between Tom and Thad and they asked me why. When we got into the discussion I knew that they needed to know the story. Of course, it was a greatly sanitized version but they do know that Rachel gave birth to Thad and that Tom is his father. They know that Tom didn't ever know."

"They haven't asked more?"

"No…I thought they would but it just hasn't happened. They asked me if they could tell Faith and I told them that they could. We haven't told Benjamin yet but he does know that I have a twin sister named Rachel."

"Whatever you do will be what's best for your family."

"What should I do with this?"

"Are you comfortable having it in the house."

Anna thought for a minute and said, "I need to show it to Ryan."

"Then let's put it in your bedroom closet for now and then let's plan a shopping trip for the girls to buy outfits for the Bar Mitzvah. We had such a good time the other times."

When the twins were Bat Mitzvah, they had all gone to Chestnut Hill Mall and shopped for most of the day. The prior year when it was Faith's turn they had gone to a mall in Cambridge and then wandered for hours in Harvard Square.

Each time the Ryan had organized an activity for the boys which included Jerry who was now Ruth's husband.

"That sounds perfect. Looking at the picture made me remember our shopping trip to Bonwit Teller and tea at the Ritz. Let's do downtown Boston this time and go for tea in one of the posh hotels."

You're on. Jerry has been asking me when we were going so he can have his day with the boys."

Jerry's own grandchildren lived out of town so it was a particular joy to him to have Anna's children so close. They adored Jerry and looked forward to the special outings he organized.

Anna vaguely remembered that she hadn't liked Jerry at first but now she couldn't remember why.

## 20

The schedule for a family of seven is busy and it was Friday night before Anna had a moment alone with Ryan. The girls were at a Shabbat retreat and the boys were watching the Red Sox game so Ryan and Anna stole away to the living room for some time alone. They each had a glass of wine and sat next to each other on the sofa chatting about the week.

Anna had placed the box with the album on the coffee table and after a while, Ryan pointed to it and asked, "I'm dying of curiosity…what is that?"

"Well…it came a few days ago. It's from Rachel."

Ryan frowned. "So that's what's been on your mind…it was Wednesday… right? You've been edgy ever since."

Anna marveled at how well her husband could read her mood.

She laughed and said, "Yes…Wednesday morning. I need you to look at this and then we need to decide what to do about it."

"Sounds ominous."

"A little but Mother has tried to convince me that it isn't threatening. I'm not sure that I trust my sister enough to believe that."

"Well...let's see."

Anna opened the box and withdrew the album and placed it in Ryan's lap. She curled up next to him and said nothing further.

Ryan inspected the album and then tentatively opened the cover. His eyes grew wide as he looked at the Bat Mitzvah photo. There were few photos of Anna and Rachel displayed anywhere-even at Ruth's house. He ran his fingers over the page and said, "You were so young."

"Same age as Thad is right now. It's our Bat Mitzvah photo."

"I've never seen many pictures of Rachel. It's eerie to see how much you look alike. It's like I am seeing double and she is your alter ego."

Anna chuckled, "That's a pleasant way to put it. I always thought evil twin."

Anna held her breath as he turned the next page. He looked closely at the photo and said, "I thought you told me you had never been to Baltimore?"

"That's just it....I haven't ever been there."

Ryan peered at the photo again and then Anna could hear his breath catch as he realized that it was a photo of Rachel and Tom.

The next few moments were completely silent as Ryan stared off into space. When he finally spoke his voice was tremulous. "Why would she send you this picture?"

"I'm not sure. Keep going."

So, with shaking hands, Ryan turned the laminated pages of the album and the saw the photos of Thad. When they came to the 9/11 memorial photo, Ryan said, "You always said that you feel her presence. This is the proof."

"I know and at first, my motherly instincts told me that I needed to protect Thad. I've always been afraid that one day she would come back for him but Mother says she doesn't think it is about that."

"Ruth has seen this?"

"Yes, I called her before I opened the box. I recognized Rachel's handwriting on the label and I was terrified."

"I don't blame you. What did Ruth say exactly?"

"Well actually we had a very frank talk about Rachel and how everything affected me as a child. I didn't know that Rachel is bipolar and has been medicated since she was in her teens. Some of the aberrant behavior has been related to her refusal to take her meds properly. I have to say that it explains a lot. And for the first time, she talked about Dad and how he had a soft spot for Rachel. It was a problem for their marriage."

"I can well imagine. Why does she think Rachel sent this album?"

"She thinks that it is her attempt to reach out to me and apologize?"

Ryan was incredulous. "By sending photos to show us that she has been stalking our son?"

"Mother thinks that it is her way of showing me my son through her eyes. A kind of love letter about Thad and a thank you to me for being his Mother."

Ryan shook his head, "Wow...that is so far from what I see. What I see makes me want to hire body guards and swear out a restraining order against her."

Anna reached out to her husband and said, "That was my reaction too. I was so horrified and frightened that I collapsed. Mother had to practically peel me off the bathroom floor but we talked about it. I am trying to take a hopeful view with this. I don't think this is a threat. I think it is Rachel's idea of a peace offering. In her whole life I never heard her give a sincere apology for anything and believe me there were many times when she owed people apologies. I don't think she knows how. This is a start."

"I have never met her so I have no frame of reference. I just know what she did to you but it's not my place to be resentful. Thad is the most amazing young man. It has been such a privilege to help raise him."

"You are the only Father he has ever known and I know that he understands that you are not his biological father but I don't think he cares. His question was idle curiosity I think. He's at an age where he is starting to see the entire world and in the course of writing his Bar Mitzvah service I think there has been some talk about his family dynamic. Of course, I would never ask but I'm fairly certain that Rabbi James has talked to him about it."

"Of course. Well…we always tell the kids to try to see the good side so we need to practice what we preach and try to be optimistic. Are you going to show this to Thad?"

That was the sixty four thousand dollar question. Anna had thought about nothing else. Her gut feeling was that the album should go back into the box and into the depths of a closet.

"Ryan, I've given this a lot of thought and I just don't see the value of sharing this with the children. If it scared us, it might terrify them. Let's put it away for now."

"I agree. I'll put it up high on a shelf in the garage…no one will find it there. I don't want to chance that the girls would find it when they are rummaging around in your closet for something to wear."

"I'll feel better if it isn't in the house."

Ryan got up from his seat and placed the album back into the box. Anna heard the door to the garage close and after a few minutes, he returned and sat down very close to her. In one smooth movement

Ryan took Anna into his arms and kissed her deeply. "I love you more than anything else in the world. I can't imagine anything happening to you and the kids. But we have to have faith….if we don't have that we don't have anything."

## 21

After that, the lead up to the Bar Mitzvah was uneventful. The girls had a trip to Copley Place, an upscale mall in Boston. Anna and Ruth lost count of the number of stores they visited or the number of outfits the girls had tried but by the end of the day, everyone declared that they had found the perfect outfit.

Exhausted by all the walking and standing, Ruth suggested that they take a cab to the Parker House for tea. It wasn't a long walk but after walking the length of the mall at least twice, she just wanted to be able to sit down.

The Parker House was an elegant old hotel and when their cab pulled up in front, the doormen helped them out of the vehicle and took their parcels for safe keeping. The interior of the hotel was plush and warm and Ruth sank into a chair. She couldn't help punctuating the move with an audible sigh.

"Granny....are you OK?" Faith asked.

"Just a little tired from all the shopping. I'm not as young as I once was. Give me a cup of tea and I'll be just fine."

"Good. I could use a rest myself." said Anna.

They sipped tea and the girls chattered on critiquing all their outfits. It was typical teenage talk filled with giggles and groans.

Anna and Ruth were content to sit back and listen to the beautiful young women talking so intimately. Although they were a blended family, it seemed to make no difference to the girls who were closer than most children born of the same parents. It was a tribute to Ryan and Anna and their fierce resolve that the children should feel universally loved.

When they felt sufficiently revived, the girls asked if they could make two more stops.

Anna laughed. She knew what was coming but she played along. "OK. Where do you want to go?"

Hannah said, "Oh...you know Mom...we always ask to go there."

"The circus?"

They all giggled and Anna said, "OK...not the circus so it must be Paris. Do you want to go to Paris for dinner?"

More giggles and Anna said, "Not Paris. I think the boys would be jealous of that so....did you girls know that Mother Goose is buried right here in Boston?"

Of course, the girls did know that but they all enjoyed the charade of pretending that it was an astounding fact.

"OK Mom but then we get to see the ducklings." Said Miriam.

So they retrieved their packages from the front desk and headed out the door. The first stop in the ritual was the Old Granary Burying Ground which was located just a few blocks from the hotel. The graveyard was the burial site for Sam Adams, John Hancock and the victims of the Boston Massacre but that held little interest for the girls who wanted to see the grave of Mary Goose, wife of Isaac Goose but most famously known as Mother Goose.

After leaving the Old Granary they strolled across Boston Common and into the Boston Public Garden to visit the Make Way for Ducklings statues. They were a small set of bronze statues near one of the entrances to the garden. There were many real ducks in the large pond that dominated the Public Garden but it was the statues that had always fascinated Anna's children.

When they got home, they found Jerry and Ryan asleep in front of the television while Thad and Ben played a video game. The coffee table was strewn with paper plates that held remnants of pizza. On the floor between the boys was a giant bowl of popcorn which they munched without looking up from their game.

The girls surveyed the room, gave a collective sigh and retreated to their rooms to look at their purchases. Anna called after them, "Fashion show in fifteen minutes."

They headed towards the twins' room and soon the sound of rattling bags and excited chatter filled the air.

Ruth and Anna flopped down on the sofa and looked at the mess. "I'll get a trash bag in a minute." Anna sighed before saying, "Hello boys...did you notice that the females of the house have returned?"

Without lifting his eyes from the screen Thad said, "Yeah. Did you have fun?"

Anna knew that he was deep in concentration and was trying to be polite so she simply said, "Yes."

Ryan opened his eyes and said, "Oh hello. You look like my wife."

Anna moved over and kissed him saying, "Good thing because I have a key to the house." She put her head on her husband's shoulder and added, "Looks like you had a good time."

Ryan yawned lazily and said, "Yes. We did. We went to the Community Center and shot some hoops and then picked up pizza on the way back. We watched some of the Red Sox game and by then Jerry and I were dozing off so the boys challenged each other to a video game. Who knows what it is but I've found that the sound is mesmerizing enough to allow a nap. I guess they made the popcorn after we were asleep."

Jerry stirred and opened his eyes and said, "Welcome home. I heard Ryan's account of the day. They wear me out!"

Ruth got up and said, "Well, I'm opening a bottle of wine."

"Great idea" said Anna as she followed her Mother into the kitchen in search of a trash bag to hold the remains of the boys' feast.


As the grownups sipped a glass of wine, the girls modeled their new finery. As they carefully described each outfit, Anna was amazed that they remembered where it had been purchased. They had been in so many stores that all she remembered was a blur of colors and fabrics.

After the fashion show, Jerry stretched his arms and said, "Well, seeing my beautiful girls modeling their new dresses gave me an appetite. What about Chinese food?"

Everyone started to laugh. Jerry loved Chinese food and he was especially fond of the food from a place that delivered to Anna and Ryan's house. He was predictable. If he and Ruth were there at meal time and no meal was in progress, he would always suggest Chinese food. Everyone would feign surprise and say what a perfect idea that would be. It was a family ritual that never ceased to entertain.

While Jerry called in the order, Anna and Ruth set the dining room table with silverware and plates. "Thanks for coming with us today, Mom."

Ruth smiled and said, "Anna, I cherish the time I can spend with your children."

Anna sighed, "They're so grown up. I'm surprised that the girls still want to spend time with me."

"Of course they do. Now don't be maudlin. The food will be here soon."

Even as a teenager, Anna had always enjoyed spending time with Ruth but after being a witness to her sister's utter rejection of her mother, she knew that there would be no guarantees with her own daughters. That's why it was important to include

Ruth in these shopping excursions and to savor all the special moments with the girls.

Soon the doorbell rang, the food was on the table and boxes of food and chopsticks were flying around the table. There were pockets of conversation but mostly they just seemed to be enjoying the food and togetherness as a family.

At the end of the meal, everyone read their fortune cookies aloud. Anna was the last and she broke the crumbly cookie open and pulled out the small bit of paper. She stared at it for a minute and said, "Forgiveness is a gift."

The room became silent for a minute and Ryan reached over and took the strip of paper from Anna's fingers. He read the words and then reached for his wife's hand.

Soon the chatter resumed and the girls started clearing away the food containers and plates. Anna and Ryan sat close to each other as they watched the flurry of activity. When the table was clear, Ruth said, "Shall I make coffee?"

Ryan looked at Anna and said, "Ruth, let's make it brandy. We'll retire to the den and let the kids clean up."

When they got to the den, Ryan opened the cabinet, pulled out a bottle of brandy and poured four snifters. He lifted his glass and said "To Chinese food and family."

No one said anything for a long time and then Anna broke the silence asking, "Do you think there's anything that's unforgiveable?"

Jerry said, "That's a hard question. As Jews we are taught forgiveness, atonement and redemption. Forgiveness is important and I think that we should be generous with it."

Anna said, "I think of myself as generous but sometimes I wonder if forgiveness is given too freely."

Ruth looked at her daughter and saw the profound pain in her eyes. "Anna, what happened with you and your sister is huge and it takes time to find forgiveness. Some people don't know how to apologize and some people don't know how to forgive but that isn't you."

"Maybe I don't want to forgive."

Ryan reached out for his wife's hand and said gently, "Well that's a whole different story but don't fool yourself, Anna. You do want to forgive. If you didn't, you wouldn't be torturing yourself with these questions."

"I know. I've held onto my hurt for so long and I realized this evening that it is so much a part of me, I am afraid to let it go but...the truth is that I forgave Tom years ago. I had to. He was my husband. And then the album came from Rachel and I tried to put myself in her place. I know that I would hope to be forgiven."

Jerry said, "Everyone always says forgive and forget but that is a lot of rubbish. We need to forgive but we don't have to forget. That doesn't mean that we carry resentment in our heart but we don't have to put ourselves in line for the same heartache again. In other words, if someone hurts us, we need to forgive but we can refuse to interact with that person again. I'm not trying to tell you what to do, Anna but it is something to think about.

"I know, Jerry.  Thank you.  Now...let's talk about something uplifting."

## 22

It was a beautiful fall day when Thad became Bar Mitzvah. Getting the Weiss-Cohen family organized to be at the temple at 10AM was a feat in itself. Anna thought it would be easier to deploy a small army. She stood in the master bedroom, wrapped in a robe as her family filed in and out with their various crises.

Hannah: Mom, which necklace should I wear?
Anna:" Your pearls."
Miriam: Mom, Can I borrow your amethyst earrings?
Anna: Yes.
Benjamin: Can I bring my Gameboy?
Anna: No.
Ryan: Which necktie should I wear?
Anna: The blue with yellow strips. Hannah:
Are you sure about the pearls? Anna: Yes.
Miriam: Mom, should I wear the sweater with my dress?
Anna: Bring it...it may be cold in the sanctuary.
Ryan: Which shoes?
Anna: Black wingtips.
Faith: Mom do you have any green eyeliner?
Anna: In my bathroom. Please use it there because I'm going to need it.

Anna felt like a general going into battle and then she realized that she had heard nothing from Thad. She looked out the window and saw him sitting on a patio chair with his ear buds plugged in. He was either listening to his Torah section again or he was listening to what Ryan called "Psych Up" music.

Regardless, he looked so grown up and so much like Tom that she could feel the tears welling up in her eyes. While she was standing there she had the oddest sensation that someone was standing next to her and she could have sworn that she smelled Tom's cologne. Chills ran through her body but then it was gone. Nerves, she thought and went over to the closet to get her dress.

Miraculously, everyone arrived at the temple on time and properly dressed. Thad led the service with poise and dignity. His Hebrew was perfect and standing there in his new blue suit he looked so much like his father it made Anna's heart ache.

Anna had known that this day would be filled with mixed emotions. The girl's Bat Mitzvah had brought back similar memories of Tom but today it was so strong. The slight smell of his cologne hung in the air and at times, Anna felt that she was hearing Tom's voice chanting the Torah.

When she and Ryan were called up to participate in blessings for Thad, she scanned the crowd in the temple and she thought that she saw Rachel. When she looked again the space was empty so she dismissed the thought and went on with the service.

After the service, they hosted a small luncheon. The real party would be later. Ryan had arranged a disco party at a local hotel.. Anna was grateful that it would be in a separate room from the adult party. She had not enjoyed the disco era and could not understand why kids wanted to recreate the ghastly music and clothing. But it was Thad's party and that's what he wanted so Ryan had taken charge.

The party would be in two adjoining rooms. The young people would be having their own separate party complete with a disco ball and flashing lights. For the adults, there would be more sedate music and soft lighting. Anna marveled at how easily Ryan had organized the event and she was looking forward to a relaxing evening with friends.

After the luncheon, Anna walked outside to the parking to get a breath of fresh air. She looked up and saw Rachel standing under a tree at the back of the parking lot.

At that moment, Anna had a choice. She could pretend to not see her sister but that would just put off the inevitable. Instead, she raised her hand to wave and Rachel walked over to her. For the first time in thirteen years, the twin sisters stood face to face.

They stared at each other. Even after all these years they still looked alike. Anna thought that Rachel had a few more wrinkles but Rachel thought that Anna looked radiant.

"He looks like Tom." Rachel said.

"He is Tom."

"Does he ever ask about me?"

"No. He knows that you are his biological mother and that you gave him to me. He's too young to understand that he looks like the twins' father. Everyone is very discreet about it but he will have questions at some point and I will try to answer them as honestly as I can."

"He didn't want me…Tom…he made a mistake and he asked me to never tell you so I haven't but…I think now is the time. I have to be able to move on. I've come here to ask for your forgiveness. I know I don't deserve it…I betrayed you and you have a right to be angry but…we are sisters…twins and I miss you. Can you find it in your heart to forgive me?

The exchange was so intense that they did not hear the footsteps come up behind them. Suddenly they heard a young man's voice say, "Mom…it's OK to forgive her. Dad would want you to."

Anna whirled around and saw that Thad was standing behind them looking quizzically at his mothers.

Anna's heart was pounding as she looked at this serious young man who was asking her to forgive the unforgiveable.

"Thad, honey, I thought you were inside."

"No…everyone is ready to go home and Dad sent me out to find you." He looked at Rachel and said, "You're my biological mother aren't you?"

Rachel said quietly, "Yes."

"I've seen you before. Do you sometimes come to my soccer games?

"Yes but I didn't know you saw me."

"You look just like my Mom….why wouldn't I notice?"

"Why didn't you say something?"

"I didn't want to."

So this was the explanation of the photos. Anna started to protest but then she heard Thad say, "Mom...I know what happened. I asked Granny a few weeks ago and she told me. She felt bad about telling me but I didn't want you to have to tell me yourself. I think it would have been too hard. You have taught us to forgive and I think you forgave her a long time ago. You just need to tell her. If I can forgive her, you should too. Don't hold onto the anger. You have loved me my whole life and taken care of me...you are my mother in every way that means anything to me. Please let it go."

It was then that Anna realized that she had forgiven Rachel. For a long time the resentment and anger filled her heart but when she met Ryan, it had slowly melted away.

Thad was right-she had forgiven Rachel but never bothered to tell her. That was her final revenge-withholding forgiveness. Her son looked at her with his deep, soulful eye-Tom's eyes- and she felt something change in her heart. Thad was asking her to let it go and as he spoke, she could hear the words in Tom's voice...let it go...please let it go.

She looked at Rachel and said, "Rachel, I forgave you a long time ago but I haven't told you. You stole something from me so I have been keeping my forgiveness from you. Yes, I forgive you. I am doing it for my son but I am also doing it for myself. Now come to the house and meet the family."

For the first time in thirteen years, the sisters hugged and then drew their son into the embrace. If they had been looking they would have seen Ruth put her head on Jerry's shoulder and weep with joy.

## ABOUT THE AUTHOR

Mary Parsons is retired from a career in the insurance industry. She is the sole caretaker for her elderly Mother. She and her dog, Spenser Banjo, live in Maine.

www.ingramcontent.com/pod-product-compliance
Lightning Source LLC
Chambersburg PA
CBHW071325130626
46556CB00004B/1750